TUNNELS
of TYRANNY

TUNNELS *of* TYRANNY

A FOURTH MOOSE JAW ADVENTURE

MARY HARELKIN BISHOP

COTEAU BOOKS FOR KIDS
WWW.COTEAUBOOKS.COM

Edited by Barbara Sapergia.
Cover illustration by Dawn Pearcey.
Cover and book design by Duncan Campbell.
Printed and bound in Canada at Transcontinental Printing.

National Library of Canada Cataloguing in Publication Data

Bishop, Mary Harelkin, 1958-
Tunnels of tyranny : a fourth Moose Jaw adventure / Mary Harelkin Bishop.

ISBN 1-55050-316-2

I. Title.

PS8553.I849T88 2005   jC813'.6   C2005-901728-7

10   9   8   7   6   5   4   3   2

COTEAU BOOKS
401-2206 Dewdney Ave
Regina, Saskatchewan
Canada   S4R 1H3

available in Canada and the US from:
Fitzhenry & Whiteside
195 Allstate Parkway
Markham, Ontario
Canada   L3R 4T8

The publisher gratefully acknowledges the financial assistance of the Saskatchewan Arts Board, the Canada Council for the Arts, the Government of Canada through the Book Publishing Industry Development Program (BPIDP), and the City of Regina Arts Commission, for its publishing program.

TABLE *of* CONTENTS

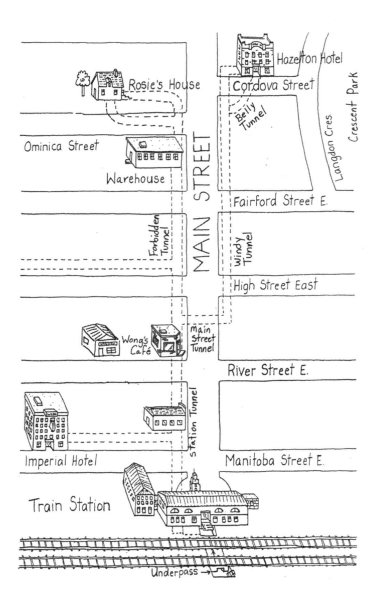

ABOVE GROUND

In loving memory of my mother,
Harriet Doreen Cojeen Harelkin

THE DRIVE

"I can't believe we're actually doing this!" Tony gripped the edge of the dashboard, fingers trembling. His freckles stood out boldly against pale skin as he peered at the torrential rain pounding the highway. Raindrops bounced at least thirty centimetres off the ground, reflecting in the headlights, making it hard to see the road ahead. "Mom and Dad are going to go ballistic!"

"I know," Andrea muttered between clenched teeth. Her hands were glued to the steering wheel as she fought to control the car. Wind buffeted the vehicle, making the windshield wipers dance a few centimetres above the glass. A semi-trailer truck heading in the opposite direction sent a curtain of rainwater blasting loudly against the car.

"Look out!" Tony yelled, throwing his body against the door as the car swerved toward the ditch.

"Don't do that!" Andrea cried as, jerking the wheel, she barely managed to stay on the road. "I'm having a hard enough time keeping control without you acting like that!"

"Who's acting?" Tony grumbled, his eyes squeezed tightly together. "I don't think we're going to get to Moose Jaw alive!"

Secretly, Andrea worried about the same thing. She slowed down even more. At this rate it would take them hours to arrive. "I'm sorry I yelled at you," she apologized, trying to relax her clenched fingers. "I'm just scared. I've never driven in a storm before."

"You've hardly driven at all," Tony reminded her grimly. "You only got your license two weeks ago! What made you think you could drive to Moose Jaw?!"

"I have to see Grandpa," Andrea whispered, blinking back the tears that had been threatening to fall ever since she'd answered the phone that afternoon. "When Aunt Bea called, she sounded so worried. I didn't know what else to do."

Tony gulped. It seemed to be raining harder than ever. He felt like they were in a car wash, there was so much water spraying around. "We should have waited for Mom and Dad," he said. "It wouldn't have been that long – just a couple of hours."

"I know," Andrea agreed, peering into the driving rain. "But what if Grandpa –" she stopped abruptly, near tears, then tried again. "I can't believe Grandpa Vance is so sick that they had to rush him to the hospital. I never thought about him getting old. He's always just been Vance to me. You know how lucky we are. We've had a really special relationship with him and Grandma and Great Aunt Bea."

"Yeah," Tony agreed, with a gentle smile. "No other kids can say that they got to travel back in time to meet their grandparents when they were teenagers."

Memories jumped into Andrea's mind like grasshoppers on a hot summer day. She saw herself as a tunnel runner, meeting her grandfather for the very first time. He had taught her all about the underground tunnels in Moose Jaw. She'd been thirteen then, suddenly thrown back into the past, and feeling very alone and afraid. As Vance, her grandfather had befriended her and protected her from the gangsters, especially Ol' Scarface. And Andrea had returned the favour when Ol' Scarface's henchmen had beaten Vance up, helping him get home safely when he was barely conscious.

The second time she had gone back in time, it had been to look for Tony, who had found a way into the tunnels alone. He'd been having a hard time dealing with his newly diagnosed diabetes, and Andrea was worried that he would forget or perhaps even decide not to take his insulin. Once back in time, they discovered that the police were causing major problems in Moose Jaw. Somehow they'd ended up right in the middle of all the trouble.

Their latest time-travel adventure had started when two of Andrea's friends had gotten dragged back in time and had to be rescued from the tunnels. Kami and Eddie Mark, Chinese Canadians, ended up as illegal immigrants in the tunnels under Moose Jaw, working as indentured servants to pay their Head Tax. That had happened just last year.

Every time Andrea and Tony ended up back in time, they got to know their grandparents a little better and now they had a very close relationship. Andrea was nowhere near ready to say goodbye to Grandpa Talbot. He couldn't die!

Tony reached over and patted her arm, pulling her thoughts back to the present. "Don't worry, it'll be okay. Doctors can perform miracles." Tony's words sounded firm and certain, but Andrea could tell he wasn't sure at all. She sent a silent prayer out the window and up into the heavy clouds hanging low over the fields: please let Grandpa be okay.

"I know doctors can work wonders," Andrea said, fighting for control of the car yet again as another huge truck whizzed by. This was crazy. She shouldn't be out here driving in this. She'd made a rash decision and now she and Tony were in a difficult and dangerous situation. Her shoulders and neck were tense and aching from the stress. Whoever said driving was fun had never driven in these conditions!

After what seemed like forever, the outskirts of Moose Jaw suddenly and magically appeared out of the darkness. Lights began to flicker through the heavy rain and Andrea breathed a sigh of relief.

"We made it!" she cried, and Tony cheered loudly. One hand at a time, she pried her stiff fingers from the steering wheel and shook them, trying to get the circulation moving again. She wanted to get out of the car and kiss the wet ground, she was so happy to be safe on Main Street in Moose Jaw. Instead, she slowed the car down for city driving and concentrated on watching the traffic lights. In a few minutes they'd be at the hospital. Grandpa had to be okay!

She drove cautiously through the rain, travelling down the long hill toward the centre of the city, deserted because of the storm. "It looks like everyone else is staying inside tonight." The train station loomed ahead like a cheery lighthouse in the rain and fog. Andrea felt a sense of calm security begin to flow through her body. Moose Jaw and the sight of the train station did that for her – it helped her feel safe. Turning left onto Fairford Street, she rolled past the spa toward the hospital.

"There it is," Tony pointed as Andrea turned into

the parking lot and found a spot close to the door.

"Thank goodness," she said, turning the car off and grabbing the keys. "We made it." She sighed, a huge sigh that helped relieve some of the tension in her body. "I'm so glad we got here safely."

"Me too," Tony agreed. "I just hope Grandpa's okay."

They had tackled one huge ordeal in the long drive through bad weather, but another one stood in their way.

WHAT'S WRONG
WITH GRANDPA?

Squaring her shoulders, mentally preparing herself, Andrea climbed out of the car. "I guess we'll find out soon enough. Let's go." Slamming the doors shut, they sprinted thirty metres across the wet pavement toward the door. Andrea's left foot landed in a hollow spot and water splashed on her running shoe.

Shaking like dogs to get rid of excess moisture, they stepped onto the black mat in front of the electronic doors. Andrea's blonde hair hung limply at her shoulders, water dripping from the ends. It ran down her neck, dampening the collar of her sweatshirt and making her shiver.

The hospital doors slid silently open and in a moment they were safe and warm in the bright interior, looking like drowned rats. "It's really coming down out there," the volunteer sitting at the information desk commented as they approached.

"We're looking for our grandfather, Vance Talbot," Andrea said. She was so focused on finding her grandfather that the woman's friendly banter didn't even register in her brain. "Can you tell us where he is, Ms., uh," she squinted, focusing on the woman's name tag, "Ms. Carrière."

Quickly Ms. Carrière wrote a number on a small square of paper and handed it over. "He's in the ICU," she said, sympathy in her voice.

"The ICU?" Tony questioned.

"That's the Intensive Care Unit, honey," she murmured, reaching out to pat his hand before she turned to help someone else.

"I don't like the sound of that," Tony said as they walked toward the elevators.

"Me either." Worry gnawed in the pit of Andrea's stomach making it difficult to swallow.

Then cold fingers wormed their way into her hand and she looked at Tony, pale and silent beside her. He didn't often hold her hand anymore, after all, he was eleven and almost as tall as she was. At least once a week he insisted they stand back to back to be measured. He ate vegetables until he was sick of them, hoping to gain a few extra centimetres. He couldn't wait to be taller than his big sister.

Like a watched pot that never boils, the elevator seemed to be taking forever. A beautiful young woman walked up and checked her watch. Little eagle feather earrings danced from her ears as she turned to push the elevator button again. Her hair was shiny and black, plaited in a single braid which hung down her back. She wore a stethoscope around her neck and green hospital scrubs, with a name tag that said "Dr. P. Greyeyes."

An Asian man, wearing thick glasses and a white lab coat, joined her just as the elevator came, and they all stepped inside. Dr. Greyeyes noticed Tony's tense face. "What are you two doing out on such a miserable night?" she asked.

"We're here to see our grandfather," Tony answered. "He's in Intensive Care."

Dr. Greyeyes patted his shoulder. "Then he's getting the best care possible. Dr. Chan," she said, gesturing toward the other doctor, "is the specialist in that area."

"Who is your grandfather?" Dr. Chan asked, his eyes full of sympathy.

"Vance Talbot," Andrea supplied, figuring she should join in the conversation.

Dr. Chan nodded. "I'll look in on him when I've done my rounds."

The elevator bumped to a stop and the doors opened, revealing an elderly woman dressed in a hot pink sweatsuit and white runners. "Andrea! Tony!" Aunt Bea dove in and practically dragged them out, hugging them both at once. Tears rolled down her cheeks. "I'm so glad you're here. He's been asking for you, Andrea." She looked behind them, puzzled. "Where are your parents?"

Andrea slipped out of the embrace. "Ah-h-h, they'll be coming soon enough, I think," she hedged, not wanting to have to explain everything right now. "Is he okay, Aunt Bea?" she asked, her brown eyes searching watery blue ones. She only wanted the truth.

Aunt Bea hesitated for a moment. "I won't lie to you," she said, clutching their hands between her clammy fingers. "He's very ill. They don't know what's wrong. He just collapsed and had to be rushed to hospital. They've been doing tests all day."

"Is he awake?" Tony wanted to know.

"He slips in and out of consciousness. Grandma is with him now. I'll go ask if you can see him." She led them down the hallway to a closed door. "Wait here." Pushing the door open, she slipped inside and disappeared, but not before Andrea caught a glimpse of flashing red lights on a heart monitor. She'd seen enough hospital shows to recognize it and it made her feel even worse.

They leaned against the wall, huddling close together for comfort. "I hate hospitals," Tony muttered, remembering the time he had had to spend in one when he was diagnosed with diabetes. "They smell funny and people die here."

Her stomach lurching, Andrea silently agreed. "But people get better, too," she gently reminded him. "You did."

"I guess so." He shrugged his shoulders in the noncommittal way that often made Andrea impatient with him. Tonight she barely noticed.

The door opened and Grandma Talbot came out. Her face was gaunt, her eyes large pools of worry. "I'm glad you're here," her voice quivered. She put frail arms around Andrea and hugged her close.

Why, I'm taller than she is, Andrea thought as her chin rested against Grandma's left temple. When had that happened? Grandma seemed to have shrunk overnight. She stood in Andrea's embrace taking comfort and strength more than offering it, and Andrea realized with a heavy heart just how old and frail her grandparents were.

"You can go in now," Aunt Bea told them. "He's resting comfortably." She opened the door and motioned for them to go ahead.

"Aren't you coming in too?" Tony hung back as if he wasn't sure he was ready for this.

Aunt Bea shook her head. "They only allow two visitors at a time, and for only five minutes." She pulled the door shut behind her, leaving them in the semi-darkness of the hospital room.

Clutching hands, Andrea and Tony moved slowly toward the bed, their wet running shoes squeaking on the waxed floor. Dim overhead lights gave the room an eerie appearance. Machines buzzed and hissed; brightly coloured lights blinked in the gloom. It felt as if they were in a dream world.

A figure lay still in the bed, tubes sticking out from under the sheet. They tiptoed closer, until their knees bumped the mattress, and stood looking down.

It doesn't even look like him, Andrea thought, tears blurring her vision. His crisp white hair was limp and oily, stark against his ashen skin. His eyelids looked thin and veiny. A clear tube was stuck under his nose and another was taped to the back of his hand.

Tony swayed and gripped the mattress with one hand, the other still caught in Andrea's grip. "Don't faint," she ordered, feeling light-headed herself.

"I-I'm scared," Tony said, his face ghostly white. "What if he dies now?" Andrea could see fine beads of sweat on his forehead. He took one more look at Grandpa Vance and then panicked, bolting out of the room.

Looking over her shoulder at the closing door, Andrea was torn. Should she follow Tony and make sure he was okay, or stay with Grandpa? As if reading Andrea's mind, Aunt Bea poked her head into the room. "I'll look after Tony," she whispered, "you stay with your grandfather." With reluctance Andrea turned back toward the bed. She didn't want to be in the room alone with him. What if something terrible happened?

"Grandpa?" she whispered. Almost of its own volition, her hand reached out. With trembling fingers she brushed his dry cheek, then smoothed his hair back from his forehead. "Grandpa, it's Andrea."

His fingers jerked and Andrea jumped. His eyes opened. "Andrea, my dear Andrea." His voice sounded hollow, as if it was taking a great effort for him to speak.

"Oh, Grandpa," she sobbed, bending forward to rest her head on his chest.

Fingers tangled in her hair. "Hush, child," his voice rasped. "I need you to listen. I need –" he gasped for breath, "you to do –"

"Anything," Andrea said, her head popping up. "I'll do anything for you, Grandpa, only just get better."

He gasped again. "You, you must go –" His voice tapered off as his eyes slid shut.

"I must what, Grandpa?" Andrea asked, gently tugging at his hand. "What must I do?"

"Get the notebook," Grandpa whispered through parched lips.

"Notebook?" she questioned, bending her ear to his lips. "You want me to get a notebook? From where? From your office?" she guessed. Her mind was already thinking of all the places he might have a notebook.

He shook his head slowly. "Back in time," he muttered, his lips having trouble forming the words. "Go back in time..."

"The notebook is back in time?! But Grandpa, that's impossible!" He must be hallucinating.

"Rosie will know," he said, choking on the words. "Go see Rosie."

"What?!" Andrea said too loudly, one hand squeezing his shoulder to wake him up. "Grandpa, what do you mean?"

"Now, now," a voice said sternly and Andrea whirled around. Nurse Stookinoff stood right behind her, her name tag vibrating on her chest as she talked. "I know you're upset about your grandfather, but you must be gentle with him. You can't yell in a hospital, you know." Taking Andrea's hand, she led her to the door. "Try to be more calm when you come back to see him in the morning."

In a daze, Andrea let herself be escorted out into the hallway, her mind running in a million directions at once. What had Grandpa been trying to tell her? What was he talking about? She couldn't go back in time just because she wanted to. It didn't work that way – did it?

"Tony is outside getting some fresh air," Aunt Bea said as she gently ushered Grandma back into the hospital room. "You two go to the house and get some sleep. There's nothing that can be done here until the morning."

Nodding, Andrea slumped against the wall as she waited for the elevator. Her knees had finally given out on her, her mind trying to take in all that Grandpa had said. Go back in time? Again? How was she supposed to accomplish that? It wasn't like she had a magic wand and could wave it every time she wanted to do a little time travelling. He wanted a notebook? What kind of notebook? He hadn't even told her that. Nothing was making any sense.

The elevator arrived and the doors slid open, allowing her to enter. Mechanically, she pushed the down button, her thoughts still spinning in her weary brain. There were too many things to worry about: Grandpa, Tony, and now a silly notebook. What did Grandpa want with it anyway? What could be in it that was so important?

"Sorry," Tony muttered when Andrea found him outside a few minutes later. He was leaning against a pole, looking weak and very pale. He watched the rain pelt down, his breath coming in steamy white puffs. "I just felt really scared all of a sudden. I guess I kind of panicked."

"It's all right," Andrea said, feeling dazed herself. "I'm afraid too." She shook her head as if that would clear her mind, still puzzled by Grandpa's bizarre request. "It doesn't make any sense," she whispered softly.

"What doesn't make sense?" Tony studied her ashen face. "Are you okay?"

"I don't know. I think I'm hallucinating. That, or else Grandpa is."

"Why? Did he talk to you?" Tony moved closer, his eyes boring into hers. "What did he want?"

Andrea shook her head again and then laughed, a strangled sound that got caught in her throat. "He wants us to go back in time!"

THE MISSION BEGINS

Andrea eased the car to a stop in front of the Talbot house and sat staring up at the familiar sight, just barely visible through the pouring rain.

"I think Grandpa has lost his mind," she said grimly, her hands squeezing the steering wheel as if it were a wet dishcloth. "You can't just say, 'Go back in time,' and then expect someone to do it! It doesn't work that way!"

"Oh, I don't know about that, Andrea," Tony disagreed. He reached into the back seat to grab his backpack. This year it had changed from the colourful kid's schoolbag he had formerly carried, into a sedate navy blue knapsack. He was growing up.

"They say that some really strange and unexplainable things can happen when people die or are near death. You know, like seeing flowers in the middle of a blizzard, or a wild animal in a strange place. And remember the first time I went back in time?" Tony queried. "I hoped and wished so much that the armoire just opened for me. They say anything is possible, if you only believe it."

"Where did you get those ideas from?" Andrea gave him a scorching look that should have sent him scurrying for cover, but Tony held his ground.

"You know how Mom is always leaving her magazines around, open to the pages she wants us to read. Well, I read one."

"And it said that?" Andrea shook her head. "Mom wanted us to read about death and spooky stuff like that?!"

"No," Tony smiled, his blue eyes twinkling mischievously. "She left it open to an article about kids watching too much TV and how bad it is. I just found the other article more interesting, that's all."

Tony stared up at the house, its rain-streaked windows dark and mysterious. "We're wasting valuable time, you know." He was obviously excited about the prospect of going back in time yet again. He had his knapsack packed with nutritious snacks and his diabetes supplies. As always, he was ready and waiting for another adventure in the tunnels!

Tony's calm acceptance of Grandpa's absurd idea helped soothe Andrea's nerves, dissipating her fears and doubts. Taking a slow, deep breath, she exhaled and looked toward the house. The front door seemed to beckon her, inviting her into its warm embrace. "I think you may be right," she whispered, feeling her fingers begin to tingle. "Maybe Grandpa does know what he's talking about. Let's go inside."

Andrea locked the car doors, pocketed the keys, and followed Tony up the wet sidewalk, trying to avoid the puddles. He sprinted ahead and had already found the hidden key that was always available for family members. He opened the door, its large window reflecting the glow from the streetlight nearby.

The door squeaked as he pushed it wide. "It feels funny," he admitted, suddenly reluctant to enter the empty house. They both stood on the porch staring down the long hallway toward the kitchen. They heard a strange humming noise and wisps of light sparkled and danced in the gloom.

"It's calling us," Andrea murmured as she made her way down the narrow hallway. The tingling sensation had already spread up her arms. A sizzling sound, not unlike the crackle of electricity, seemed to pulse in the air. Pale green and pink ribbons of light danced in the hallway like the northern lights. "It's almost exactly like it was when we went back in time last year, remember?"

"See, I told you," Tony whispered. "The armoire is open and waiting for us. Let's go!"

Nodding, Andrea took charge, gently nudging Tony behind her. "It looks like you're right," she agreed. He was smarter and more mature in some ways than he had been the previous year, she realized, but he was already caught up in the excitement of going back in time. He had forgotten about the real reason for this time-travel visit.

"Okay," she told him sternly, barring his way into the kitchen, a serious look on her face, "listen to me, Tony. You've already forgotten why we're going back in time!"

He gulped and nodded, a guilty expression settling on his features. "Yeah, I guess I did."

Andrea took pity on him and her voice softened. "It's okay, Tony, but let's remember why we're going. We can't get caught up in visiting with everyone. We have a serious job to do. We don't know why this notebook is so important to Grandpa Talbot, but it is, and we have to find it. And we can't tell anyone that Grandpa Vance is sick, either."

"We can't? Why not?"

"I just don't think it's a good idea. Think about it for a minute. Would you want to know that on June 25, 2057, you're going to be in a car accident and be really hurt?"

Tony thought about it for a moment then shook his head. "No, I guess not."

"I wouldn't either, and I just don't think we should say anything about Grandpa. Okay?"

She waited a moment while Tony thought it over. "Okay," he agreed.

"So, here's the plan. We're going to get that notebook and get back to the present then back to the hospital as soon as we can. You know, Grandpa's life may depend on it."

Tony turned pasty white. "I didn't think of it like that. That's really scary."

"I just hope I can pretend everything's okay here," Andrea said. "I'm afraid I'll burst into tears the minute I see Vance."

"No you won't," Tony comforted, patting her shoulder. But secretly he was worried about the same thing. "We can do this, Andrea," he said, trying to convince them both. "Remember what you said. Grandpa's life might depend on it."

Wiping the tears from her face, Andrea gave her brother a hug. "We have to really help each other out on this one. This will be our toughest trip ever. I don't like the idea of keeping secrets from Vance and Beanie and everyone, but we have to."

"Me either," Tony agreed. "Big secrets like this sort of eat a hole in my stomach. They make me feel sick all the time."

Smiling, Andrea nodded. "I know exactly what you mean, but we have to do it this time. It's for the best." They nodded at each other in agreement. "Well, I guess we'd better go now. The sooner we go, the sooner we can find that notebook and get back here. I just wish I had different clothes to wear."

She looked down at her blue jeans and white sweatshirt, emblazoned with a huge moose and the words "I ♥ Moose Jaw." It had been a gift from Grandpa and Grandma. "Oh well, what's important is that we get there and back as fast as possible."

"Yeah," Tony said. "Maybe there's a secret cure for whatever Grandpa has. Maybe that's what's in the notebook."

"Maybe," Andrea said. Turning left, she walked the few steps over to the basement door and pulled. The doorknob vibrated in her hands, that familiar tingling sensation making her fingers twitch. Together she and Tony walked down the stairs, already feeling invisible coils of time wrapping around them.

The office door was open, lights shimmering around it and spilling out into the basement. Their feet kept moving, as if they were caught in a tractor beam pulling them ever closer to the tunnel entrance hidden behind the armoire in Grandpa's office.

The armoire already stood open and away from the wall, the black tunnel seeming to reach out toward them. "Here we go," Andrea said, as they were guided gently into the dark void behind the large wooden cupboard. "Hold my hand –"

Her words were lost as the humming increased in volume. Lights began to pulsate. Andrea turned to watch as the armoire swung shut, locking them in a no man's land of time. She knew from past experience that the door would only open when it was ready to accept them back into the present.

It was unnerving to think that an inanimate object had such power and control. She always worried that they might get stuck in the past forever, and this time that worry sat on her heart like a stone. If they were stuck in the past, they would never see Grandpa again, even if they did find the notebook.

Andrea's world began to spin and she turned around, putting the armoire and those anxious thoughts out of her mind. Unidentifiable objects seemed to be zooming past them at enormous speeds. The world tilted back and forth, making her dizzy. One second she was standing on her head, the next she felt as if she was flying through space! She closed her eyes, hoping the feeling would go away. Her whole body tingled and throbbed, especially her fingers and toes, and her hair felt as if it were standing on end.

Gradually things began to slow down. The tingling sensation left Andrea's legs. Her eyes cleared and she found herself still clutching Tony's hand, standing in the now familiar claustrophobic darkness of a tunnel. It stretched back behind them to the sealed armoire and forward for a short distance before it curved, joining another tunnel.

A lantern was flickering faintly in the darkness, hanging from a nearby post. "We made it," Andrea announced, looking around.

"All right!" Tony shouted, doing his little dance. "Look, there's a lantern and it's lit! We're back in the past!" Then he remembered. "Sorry," he apologized, looking chagrined. "I keep forgetting that we're on a mission this time."

"Oh, Tony, it's okay to be happy, just don't get too carried away," Andrea sighed.

Andrea was happy too, in a strange kind of way. If only Grandpa weren't so sick! If only they didn't have to find that notebook! Then she could really enjoy her trip to the past. She felt so bewildered. Her emotions were seesawing back and forth like a ride at the amusement park. One moment she felt like she was on the verge of tears, the next she was smiling, remembering some endearing thing Grandpa had said. It was all too confusing and emotionally exhausting. She knew from experience, though, that she would never rest until she had the notebook safely in her hands. It felt as if that might be Grandpa's only hope for survival.

"Let's go now," she said, taking charge. "We don't have a minute to lose."

"I'm glad to see all the lanterns are lit," Tony commented, looking down the narrow tunnel. "We've come back to the same place we always do, in the little tunnel near Rosie's house. It looks like things aren't as bad as they were the last time we were here."

"I hope you're right." Andrea stared down the familiar tunnel. She knew it led to a slightly larger tunnel which ran north and south, connecting Rosie's house and the storage area. The Forbidden tunnel was attached to the other end of the storage area and led to the train station.

Knowing about the tunnels gave Andrea a calm sense of control, something she hadn't felt since she'd answered the phone so many hours before. "Let's walk to the end of the tunnel and head up to Rosie's place. She'll know all about that notebook, Grandpa said so." Turning north toward Rosie's would take them away from downtown Moose Jaw and most of the tunnels, but Rosie's was where they wanted to go first.

"Sounds good to me." Tony let Andrea lead the way, grinning in the semi-darkness. Stretching his hand out, he touched the dirt walls, enjoying the feeling of his fingers bumping over the uneven surface. It made him confident that he was really here.

Tony was worried about Grandpa too, but he was sure glad to be back in time. He couldn't wait to see the looks on Rosie's and Beanie's faces when they saw him! He bet he was even taller than Beanie now!

Andrea was so anxious that she barely registered that usual feeling of claustrophobia rising in the pit of her stomach. Maybe after so many trips in the tunnels, she was finally used to the feeling of the dirt walls closing in around her. Then a small scurrying noise sounded from above and Andrea's neck disappeared into her shoulders in a second. On the other hand, maybe she'd never get used to being underground.

A louder and more distinct sound echoed through the passageway. Andrea lurched to a halt, her feet skidding on the gravel. Tony crashed into her from behind. "Hey! What was that?"

"Sh-h-h," Andrea warned. They stood stock-still in the middle of the tunnel while the unmistakable sound of voices and marching feet floated toward them.

"It sounds like an army down here," Tony whispered. "What do you think is happening?"

"I don't know." There was no point in whispering. Whoever was making all that noise would never hear their conversation. "I think it's coming from the storage area."

"Let's go investigate," Tony said, excitement in his voice, but Andrea grabbed his arm, holding him back.

"I don't think that's a good idea. We don't know who it is or what they're doing. We might walk into something really bad."

"I guess you're right." Tony scuffed his feet in the gravel, visions of adventure evaporating before his eyes.

The sounds seemed to grow louder and more frenzied as Andrea and Tony approached the intersection of the tunnels. It sounded to Andrea like the busy activities of the opening night of a play. Excitement and anticipation hung in the air along with agitated voices and nervous laughter.

At the intersection, Andrea cautiously stuck her head around the corner and then jerked it back in again. She slammed her body into an indentation in the dirt wall, gesturing wildly for Tony to do the same thing. "Someone's coming," she whispered hoarsely. "Hide, quick."

Tony planted himself against the rough wall on the opposite side of the tunnel, pressing his body into a slight recess in the dirt. Little pebbles and soil rained down upon them, helping them blend into the tunnel walls.

A strange swishing noise swooped through the tunnel as a flash of white sped by the entrance. It stopped in plain sight, whirled around and then went back toward the storage area. "What was that?!" Tony whispered in fear.

"I don't know." Andrea felt her heart thumping in her chest, her mind conjuring all sorts of frightening visions.

For several moments they were silent, frozen to their spots in disbelief. Then Andrea admitted her worst fears. "It didn't even look human, did it?"

Tony gulped, shaking his head. "It had a long pointy head and black holes for eyes."

Andrea wanted to deny it, but she couldn't. That was exactly what she'd seen, too. Could two people have the same illusion?

"Do we believe in ghosts?" Tony's voice was faint and small.

"No," Andrea said firmly, pushing the frightful images out of her mind. "There's no such thing as ghosts." But she wasn't so sure, not after what they'd just witnessed.

"What are we going to do now?" Tony asked, still firmly plastered against the tunnel wall, his knees shaking. The nylon buckles of his knapsack were digging painfully into his back, but he kept the pressure on. He was so afraid, he knew that if he tried to move any part of himself his legs would give out and he'd end up on the ground. "I don't want to be here anymore. This place is haunted!"

"We can't go into the storage area, that's for sure. It sounds like there's a party going on in there! And there's no point in trying to open the armoire. It seems to have a mind of its own. We'll just have to take our chances heading up this tunnel to Rosie's and hope no one is coming in the opposite direction."

"That's not very reassuring," Tony commented, his voice as dry as the dust that stirred beneath their feet. "Especially since that – that thing went down there just now."

Silently Andrea agreed with him. Out loud she put

on a brave front. "Come on," she cajoled him. "What are the chances it will come back any time soon?" The words were barely off her lips and into the air when the same swishing sound caught their attention again. The air seemed to flow around them, getting colder.

"It's coming back." Tony mouthed the words, as his knees gave out. He thumped to the ground and buried his head in his hands.

"No, I think there are two of them!" Andrea kept her eyes pinned on the tunnel intersection, hoping to catch a better glimpse of the thing, whatever it was. She just hoped it wouldn't see her. What if it turned its head at the last second and spotted them? She didn't even want to think of that possibility. Her heart pounded uncontrollably in her chest, feeling like it would explode, and she concentrated on inhaling slowly and deeply.

Another figure flew by, a blur of white, the swishing noise just as loud. It, too, did a little twirl and then glided back toward the storage area. This one was large and funny-looking in a sinister way, which sent chills racing up and down her spine. What were they doing, putting on a ghoulish fashion show?! It was bizarre!

"Let's get out of here," Tony whispered, his voice quaking with fear. "That was a ghost!"

"It was not a ghost," Andrea argued, although she wasn't totally convinced.

"Yes it was," Tony breathed, rushing across the tunnel and gluing himself to her side. "It was all white and shimmery, even its head! And did you see the eyes! Let's get out of here before they come back!" Too frightened to wait, Tony burst around the corner and into the larger tunnel, running at full tilt.

"Tony!" Andrea called, but not too loudly. She didn't want to be heard. Had that been a ghost? In all of her adventures in the tunnels, she had never once thought about the idea of a ghostly presence haunting them. She had to force herself not to race after Tony. What good would that do?

Willing herself to be calm, she stepped into the larger tunnel. It ran north and south, leading from the underground storage area to the tunnel entrance at Rosie's house. A whisper of rustling reached her ears, or was she imagining it?

Fear began to tickle the back of her neck, causing the tiny hairs to stand at attention. Noises could still be heard echoing from the storage area. Would ghosts make that much noise? Curiosity finally galvanized her into action. Eyes straining, she stared toward the underground cavern, wondering what was going on.

Yellow light from the lanterns danced wildly, sending black freakish shadows against the earthen walls. Was this some kind of ghostly ritual? She thought she heard a low mournful sound coming toward her. The very idea gave her the creeps and shuddering, she broke into a run, calling, "Tony! Wait for me!"

Back In Time

Fear chased Andrea through the tunnel, nipping at her heels. Where was that hidden door? Where was Tony?

Finally she spied the tunnel door, just swinging shut. Leaning into it, she pushed with all she had, sending it careening loudly into the wall. As she went through the door, something warm and soft touched her hand and she jumped, hitting her head on the wooden frame, stifling a strangled cry.

"It's just me," Tony gasped.

"Don't do that!" Andrea said, her words sounding harsh. "You scared me to death!"

"Well, I'm scared, too," Tony pointed out. "Let's get out of here!"

Racing on, they came upon a second door within

seconds. This door opened easily and led to the stairs of the outside cellar entrance to Rosie's house. Above them, lying at an angle veering away from the house, lay the heavy wooden door. "We're almost there," she panted, her voice strained. "I'm so glad."

Mounting the stairs, Andrea let her shoulders rest against the underside of the big door. She climbed up another step, the door creaking as it opened a crack. Fresh air spilled into the cellar entrance; it smelled safe and normal. She took deep breaths trying to calm herself.

"That thing we saw..." Tony said. "Did you see its eyes?"

"Yes, I did," Andrea replied. The figure in the tunnel had been all white, its eyes black, leering holes. Could it really have been a ghost?

"It sounds busy above-ground, too," Tony observed, pressing his ear to the crack. "Like everyone's getting ready for a party or something. I can hear cars driving by – lots of them! And horses, too! Something big is happening!" He pressed his eye against the crack and peered out.

"Is it safe for us to go out?" Andrea asked with a grunt. The door was getting heavy.

"Well, safer than staying in here, I'd say. Come on, push!" Putting his hands over his head, he helped Andrea open the door and together they stepped out into the excitement of the night.

They quickly closed the cellar door and looked around. "Yep, we're back in the 1920s again," Tony surmised, looking at the houses, listening to the horses and carriage wheels. He let the idea of ghosts slip from his mind. "Let's go find our relatives!"

Together they sprinted out of the backyard and around the side of the house to the front yard. They were heading up the steps to the porch when the door banged open and Beanie careened across the wide porch. "Beanie!" Andrea called. She and Tony sprinted up the steps to the porch and the three fell into an embrace.

"Andrea! Tony!" Beanie took turns hugging them, giggling and grinning from ear to ear. Her happiness was contagious and they all danced in a circle, arms entwined.

"You've grown," Andrea commented as they stepped back to look at one another, wide grins on their faces. Beanie was as tall as Tony, her blonde hair cut and styled into a bob that curled under just below her ears.

"Yes," she replied with obvious disgust. "Look what my mother is making me wear now!" Pinching the offending garment with the thumb and forefinger of each hand, she turned her shoulders this way and that, modelling a long-waisted blue-and-white striped dress.

"You look very nice," Andrea said diplomatically, biting back a smile. She knew how much Beanie hated to have to act grown-up.

"You look like a girl!" Tony added, his disappointment evident. Maybe Beanie wouldn't want to go on adventures with him anymore.

Shrugging her shoulders, Beanie sighed. "Well, there's not much I can do about that! Anyway, what are you two doing here? I'm so glad to see you!"

"There's no time for idle chit-chat now," Rosie called from an old-fashioned automobile idling noisily at the curb, its large-spoke wheels gleaming. "I'm glad to see you too, but we have a job to do. We have to get to the rally. Come on!"

"Rosie, are you driving?" Tony asked, hurrying across the yard to give the car a closer inspection. "Wow! I can't believe this thing actually runs!"

"What do you mean?" Rosie snorted. "It's the latest model. My cousin broke his leg last week and he'll be laid up all summer. He said I could use his automobile!"

"Oh yeah," Tony reminded himself, he was back in time!

"This car is the cat's meow," Beanie added, climbing carefully into the back seat, so as not to muss her dress.

"Cat's meow?" Tony mouthed, moving in to sit beside her. He wrestled out of his backpack, placing it on the floor at his feet.

"That means it's a great car, Tony," Andrea interpreted, running around to the driver's side of the car to give Rosie a big hug. "They use that expression like we say 'cool' or 'super.'"

"So if you said, 'This is a cool car,' you'd mean it was special?" Beanie asked, frowning. "Sometimes you talk so strangely."

The door to the house banged open again and Vance strode out carrying a large camera and tripod, a scowl on his face. Spotting two extra bodies in the back seat, he stopped short, staring. "Andrea, Tony," he said by way of greeting, when he recognized them. He sounded gruff and businesslike, not at all his usual cheery self.

"If you want to come with us, that's fine, but Rosie and I have a story to write. Don't get in our way." He settled himself in the front seat, leaning the legs of the tripod against the seat.

"He's grumpy these days," Beanie whispered, as Rosie revved up the engine. "He got a job as a newspaper reporter, but he's having trouble writing stories they'll accept. I'm worried about him and so is Sarah."

So am I, Andrea thought. Blinking back tears, she remembered the condition Grandpa was in when she had left him behind, sick in the hospital.

As if on cue, a friendly, "Yoo-hoo," was heard coming from the direction of the house. Andrea saw Sarah leaning out of the upstairs window, waving a white dishcloth. Baby Alan's head was just visible above the bottom of the window, his little hand wildly waving.

"Hi Sarah! Hi Alan!" Andrea and Tony called in chorus. "We'll talk as soon as we get back."

"Where are we going?" Andrea asked.

"Yeah," Tony echoed, gawking at all of the old-fashioned cars driving by. "What's going on?"

"We're not too sure," Rosie replied lifting herself off the seat and adjusting a big pillow behind her. "It's a big rally being held just out of town and everyone is invited to attend."

"What's with the pillow?" Tony wondered. "I've never seen anyone drive with a pillow before."

"I'm too short for the pedals," Rosie told him, wriggling to mould the pillow into a comfortable shape at her back.

Tony rolled his eyes. "Well, just adjust the seat then."

Andrea's elbow found his ribs and he grunted. "Oh yeah, they probably don't have that luxury in this car."

"They don't," Andrea said flatly. "We're lucky there's a front windshield!"

"Anyway," Rosie continued, stretching her legs toward the pedals. "Some strange and unsettling events have happened in Moose Jaw and we have to figure out what it's all about."

"And we need to write about it," Vance added, slouching in the seat, his arms folded across his chest. "Let's get a move on. We haven't got all day."

His obvious bad mood bothered Andrea and she didn't know what to make of it. She had never known her grandfather to be moody. Her mind slipped to the present and a picture of Grandpa Talbot, sick and struggling for breath, flashed through her mind.

"Just give me a minute," Rosie complained, adjusting the pillow one more time.

"Well, let's hope this isn't a repeat of the last drive we took with you," Vance sighed. "I was the one who had to go back and repair the fence."

"You hit a fence?" Tony turned large eyes toward Andrea. "Maybe we should walk." Feeling around on the seat, he turned to Andrea. "They don't even have seat belts!"

"Of course not," she admonished. "I don't think seat belts were invented until the 1950s."

"Maybe I should drive," Vance added. "At least I can reach the pedals!"

"I have to learn to do this properly," Rosie grunted. Her pillbox hat had slipped to one side and she reached up to set it firmly on her head, then gripped the large steering wheel with two hands and gunned the engine.

"Hang on to something," Beanie advised, gripping the edge of the car with two hands.

Rosie ground the gears loudly and the automobile lurched toward the fence. "Watch out!" Vance yelled, reaching over and grabbing hold of the wheel. He cranked it in the opposite direction and the car veered into the street, bouncing merrily.

"I guess they don't know much about shocks yet." Tony's voice shuddered with every bounce as his hands clamped onto the edge of the seat. "A person could get tossed out of the car!" He pictured himself sailing over the back seat and into the middle of the road behind them. It wasn't a pretty picture.

They drove west up Ominica Street then turned on First Avenue. "Hey! That looks like Mr. Wong," Tony said, pointing to the figure of a man dressed in a long black trench coat and derby hat. "It is him," he confirmed as they rolled closer. "Let's stop and say hello."

"Mr. Wong," Rosie greeted as the car lurched to a stop beside him.

"What brings you out here just now?" Vance asked. He had noticed the worried look on Mr. Wong's face.

"Hello, my friends," Mr. Wong greeted, his mouth barely pulling into a smile, although he noticed Tony sitting in the back seat. "I have some bad news."

"What is it?" Rosie asked, leaning toward him. "Where are you going?"

Mr. Wong pulled a piece of paper out of the breast pocket of his business suit. "I am going to the police station with this." He handed it to Vance.

Opening up the folded piece of paper, Vance read it aloud. "Beware, Coolie. You are in danger! Take your family and your business out of this town or else..."

"I am usually not frightened by such things," Mr. Wong admitted, looking embarrassed, "but I am worried for my wife and children. I do not want anything to happen to them." He paused and then softly added, "Especially after what happened with the laundry business on the corner." He pointed down the street to the corner of Main and Ominica.

"What happened?" Rosie asked, her voice full of concern.

"Why, they were forced out of their building and sent out of town. The men came one night and removed them from the premises."

"What?!" Vance was shocked. "Why didn't the police do anything?"

Mr. Wong shook his head sadly. "They were never told of this, I'm afraid. The Chinese people who owned the business were too afraid and wouldn't report it. I am not afraid. I have many friends here, I hope."

"Of course you do," Tony asserted, reaching out to pat Mr. Wong's shoulder. "You have me."

Mr. Wong smiled. "Thank you, young Tony. I am very glad to see you. I hope you will come by my café soon so that we may have a proper visit. Now, I must hurry to the police station and you must get on your way."

"Yes, we must," Rosie agreed, preparing to drive away. "We'll be in touch, Mr. Wong," she said. "I want to get to the bottom of this."

He bowed, pressing his hands to his chest. "Thank you, my friends."

They watched him walk away. "What's going on?" Tony asked, puzzled.

Rosie sighed, shaking her head. "I don't know, but I'm going to find out."

"I think it might have something to do with this rally we're going to," Vance said. "Look how many people are going."

A steady stream of cars and buggies drove by. "It looks like everyone's heading out of town," Vance muttered darkly, watching the parade of vehicles, each one piled high with people. "I sure would like to know what's going on."

Rosie eased the car into the traffic. "We know it's some kind of rally for something called the Klan. We saw a flyer advertising it."

"The Klan?" Andrea repeated, sure that she had heard that expression before.

"Do you think it might have something to do with ghosts?" Tony asked. He shuddered, moving closer to Andrea.

"Ghosts?" Vance turned in the seat to study him more closely. "What's this about ghosts?"

"Well, I think we saw some in the tunnels just now. Tall white figures with really scary eyes and pointy heads."

"That's interesting." Taking out a notebook, Vance

flipped it open and began jotting something down. "We've heard other people describe that same creature. They've been spotted throughout Moose Jaw. They seem to disappear as quickly as they come."

When Andrea spied the notebook, she gasped, then quickly covered the sound with a little cough. Was that the one Grandpa had sent her to get? She stared hungrily at its thin black cover, searing it into her memory.

"So you think we did see a ghost?" Andrea quickly asked to cover her surprise about the notebook. She tapped Vance on the shoulder from the back seat, trying to get his attention. He continued to scribble notes into his book.

"We don't know what's going on," Rosie sighed. "There's never a dull moment in Moose Jaw, that's for sure. First gangsters, then illegal activities by the lawmen, then bad treatment of the Chinese people, and now mysterious white figures stirring up trouble and upsetting people. You know, I heard that some of the Ukrainian people in Garlic Heights were being harassed too."

"Garlic Heights?" Andrea questioned. "I've heard that before."

"That's what some people call the part of town south of the creek. That's where many of the Eastern European people live."

"The who?" Tony asked, wondering what Rosie was talking about.

41

"You know, the Ukrainians and Romanians and Hungarians. Sometimes when they come downtown to do business they get heckled and harassed by other people. I don't understand it. It's as if people are afraid of anyone whose skin is different or who eat different foods, like garlic – hence the name Garlic Heights."

She braked abruptly as the procession came to a sudden halt. "Sorry everyone," she apologized as the three heads in the back seat jerked forward and then bounced back against the seat. "Everyone seems to be heading out of town for this event tonight."

"Yeah, this is the most exciting thing that's happened in Moose Jaw in a long time," Beanie smiled, clapping her hands together. "I love excitement!"

"Well, ghosts or no ghosts," Vance said, slapping his notebook closed, "we're going to get to the bottom of this!"

THE RALLY

"I've never seen so many cool vehicles," Tony said as their car joined the long procession of Model T-type cars and horse-drawn carts heading out of town.

"It looks like the whole town is here," Andrea stated. "I didn't know old Moose Jaw had so many people! It reminds me of when everyone in the city is going to a rock concert back in our time."

"What's a rock concert?" Beanie asked. "Do people bring special rocks and hit them to make music?"

Andrea and Tony laughed. "It's like a big party," Tony said, joining Beanie to wave and call out greetings to passengers in other vehicles. "It's a music concert."

"These people can't all be from Moose Jaw," Andrea decided, watching wagon after wagon drive by overflowing with people.

"You're right," Vance told her. "They come from all over the place, including Alberta and Manitoba."

"They even have special trains bringing hundreds of people from Regina," Rosie informed them, gritting her teeth as she gazed straight ahead, her eyes riveted on the horse-drawn cart moving slowly in front of her.

It took over an hour to drive the few miles west of town to the meeting place. The sun, fire red, hung on the western horizon, casting long shadows across the grass. "It looks like there are a million cars and buggies parked on the grass," Tony exaggerated, pointing to the sea of vehicles parked in long rows.

"More like a hundred," Vance muttered, jotting this fact down in his notebook as Rosie pulled up beside a bigger car with a rumble seat pulled down in back.

"And look at all the people," Beanie added. "I've never seen so many people in one place in my whole life."

"We'll all stick together," Rosie informed them, climbing out of the car. "Something doesn't feel right about this meeting, and I don't want to lose anyone out here, especially when it gets dark. It's a long walk home."

"But some people are walking," Tony pointed out. "It looks like everyone wants to be in on this rally."

Vance grabbed the camera and tripod and struggled to get them out of the car. "Let's find a spot close to the front so I can get a good photograph."

"Which way is the front?" Andrea asked, for there

seemed to be wall-to-wall people fanning out in every direction, talking excitedly. Some had spread blankets and sat on the ground as if they were at a picnic.

"I'd say that's the front." Vance pointed to a large structure reaching high into the sky.

"That's a cross," Rosie said, her lips pinched in a frown. "I wonder what they want with that."

People milled about in groups, talking and laughing as they waited. It had the atmosphere of a carnival and Andrea wouldn't have been surprised to find people setting up little booths and selling things.

They meandered through the crowds, trying to stay together. "Remember where the car is parked," Vance called back. "If we get separated, meet back at the car afterward."

Andrea ploughed ahead, trying to keep up with Vance. She wasn't sure she'd be able to find the car, if she got separated. They all looked alike to her, big and black and old-fashioned. Thank goodness someone had invented coloured paint for cars!

"Just wait for us, Vance," Rosie ordered, puffing as she skirted a group of men smoking cigars and telling jokes. "We're right behind you."

Vance muttered under his breath and set the camera on the ground. "He sure has a bee in his bonnet these days," Beanie offered, still holding Andrea's hand. "Even Sarah has a hard time jollying him out of his bad moods."

"What's the problem?" Andrea asked. She was worried about this Vance and Grandpa at the same time.

"Do you remember Jack?"

Andrea nodded. "I remember." He was the boy who had helped her and Vance get jobs as delivery boys in the laundry where her friend Kami had been held captive. Jack had come to her rescue a couple of times, once at a very crucial time. She owed him a lot and wondered if she would be able to see him and thank him properly.

Dragging Andrea to a stop, Beanie reached up and cupped her hand around her ear. "Jack was shot about two months ago."

It took a moment or two for the words to register. "What?!" Andrea almost shouted.

"Sh-h-h," Beanie warned. "There's more." Pulling Andrea down, she whispered, "No one knows who shot him. They called it a gang-style shooting, you know, like they have in Chicago. Whoever did it left him to die behind the Hazelton Hotel. There were rumours about him getting in with the wrong crowd and making someone mad."

"Someone like Mean-Eyed Max?" Tears filled her eyes as she thought of poor Jack.

"Sh-h-h," Beanie told her, pressing cold, clammy fingers against Andrea's lips. "We don't even mention that name around here anymore, though I've heard rumours that he's been seen on River Street. I thought he'd be in jail for a lot longer than that!" Andrea shivered.

"Anyway, Vance has never been the same since then. He's taking Jack's death pretty hard." Beanie looked up and found that they were surrounded by strangers and that Vance had moved along. "Hey! Where did everyone go?"

They searched the crowds and finally spotted Tony waving wildly at them. "This way!" he called, jumping up and down to be seen over the throng of people. They made their way to the others and collapsed to the ground.

Vance had already set the camera up on the tripod. The piece of black material draped over it gave it a sinister look.

"It's almost time to start," Tony informed them, pointing to a couple of businessmen standing on the makeshift stage. They were dressed in black suits with black derby hats. Glancing around the crowd, he noticed that every man present was wearing some kind of hat! Most were black; some were tan or grey with a black band around the crown.

The women wore hats as well, some of the funniest-looking hats Tony had ever seen! The woman standing next to him had what looked to be a squashed, lilac-coloured army helmet pulled low over her eyes. It had a large yellow feather attached on either side. Stifling a giggle, he turned around. And his grandma thought modern kids dressed funny!

One of the men on stage called for attention and a hush fell over the crowded field. Andrea was amazed that that many people could get so quiet that quickly. Without the aid of microphones, the man began to speak, and again she was surprised. Everyone seemed to be able hear him!

"Good evening, ladies and gentlemen," he began, his voice booming over the crowd. Even in the fading light and even though he was wearing a hat, Andrea could see that the man had flaming red hair and a fiery red moustache. "Carrot top," Grandma Talbot called that hair colour.

"My name is Red Thompson." he continued, his voice a rich, deep bass that rang confidently over the crowd. "Allow me to introduce some of the other people on stage with me tonight. This is Ted Rogers," he said, pointing to the person standing beside him, a man of average build, with thin, greying hair and a crooked smile.

"And this is Mr. James Robertson and his lovely wife Esther." Mr. Robertson was big and burly, like a football player, with thick, horn-rimmed glasses. His wife looked tiny and delicate as she smiled into the crowd.

There was shuffling and a few moments of confusion as the people on stage stepped to the back and stood in a line. Red Thompson stepped forward and the crowd fell silent once again.

As soon as he began to speak, Andrea felt chills chase up and down her spine. Red Thompson smiled and looked friendly enough, but his words sounded as if they had hidden meaning. She had to listen carefully, for he seemed to be talking in riddles. He said something about this being the first meeting of a growing organization, and how happy he was that so many people had chosen to attend. He talked about the objectives of the group and how the group members wanted one Canada, with one language, and more opportunities for its people.

Something didn't sound right, but Andrea couldn't figure out what it was. She listened while the crowd around her clapped and cheered heartily. "We are the Klan," she heard the speaker shout above the applause. It was the same word Rosie and Vance had used and again it stirred some forgotten memory. Where had she heard it before?

Red Thompson wiped his sweating forehead with a large handkerchief and announced that Mr. Robertson would now speak. There was a polite smattering of applause as he stepped to the front of the stage. James Robertson talked about the Klan in the United States and how it had a membership of 40,000. He was obviously looking for recruits.

"Our offices are in the warehouse on the corner of Main Street and Ominica. We have...ah-h-h..." He hesitated for a moment as if he was carefully thinking of which words to use. "We have rented the building," he finished.

"Hey! That's the warehouse he's talking about!" Tony pointed out.

"That's right!" Andrea suddenly remembered. "That's where the Chinese laundry was! That's the building and business Mr. Wong was talking about!"

Mr. Robertson waited until an even deeper hush had fallen over the crowd. "Well, let's just say that we want equal opportunities for *our* people," he emphasized the word "our," looking out over the crowd. "We have dispensed with the Chinese laundry business. That building is ours now."

He pumped a beefy-looking fist in the air. "We want our people to have the advantages that this nation can provide without having to compete with the cool – uh, the Chinese or the Jewish people, or the Catholics, for that matter. We want a pure race!"

Andrea mulled over his words, a sick feeling spreading in the pit of her stomach. This didn't sound very good at all. There was something unsavoury about this Klan organization; they sounded prejudiced against everyone but themselves!

"Membership in our group is a mere ten dollars."

"Ten dollars?" Andrea heard someone gasp. "That's steep."

The speaker must have heard that remark, for he hurriedly added, "With a ten-dollar membership, you get a handsome uniform as well. Many of our members are wearing them tonight."

"Let's see them!" The crowd began to call. "Show us the uniforms!"

There was a quick discussion between the two main speakers and then Red Thompson waved to a group of people standing to the far left of the stage. There was a thump of boots on wood as several people mounted the stairs. An odd hush fell over the crowd and then a collective gasp filled the air.

"Ghosts!" A child's voice cried. "I see ghosts!"

MEET THE KLAN

Several children began to cry in fear. Andrea stared at the strange uniforms while Vance scrambled under the black cloth to get his photograph. They were the most outlandish costumes she had ever seen. And yet they looked familiar.

Each uniform consisted of a long white tunic with loose bell sleeves. Two large crests were attached, one on each shoulder. That part of the costume didn't look too bad, but it was the hat, or actually, hood, which gave the outfit its bizarre appearance. It was long and pointed like a witch's hat, made of white material which covered the head. It draped over the chest and shoulders. The peak rose about thirty centimetres above the wearer's head. Two gaping eyeholes were cut out of the material. It was these that gave the uniform its ghostly appearance.

"My land," Rosie muttered, looking as if she was going to swoon. "What is the world coming to? Baby Alan would be terrified. I'm glad he's not here to see this."

Vance's flash pan flared as he took a photograph. "I hope this turns out. I can't wait to write this article!" He flipped furiously through his notebook and began taking notes. "Sh-h-h, the speaker's talking."

A hush fell over the crowd once again and Mr. Robertson continued. "Our objective is racial purity," he stated, his voice ringing with authority. "We believe there should be a ban on marriages between white women and Negroes, Chinese, and Japanese men."

"They can't tell you who you can marry," Beanie insisted, her eyes flashing with anger. "That isn't right."

"It's nobody's business," Rosie agreed, making quick notes and then scanning the crowd, assessing their reaction. "I wonder how many new members they'll get after tonight?" A worried expression settled on her face.

Mr. Robertson continued over the murmuring in the crowd. "We must stop racial impurity. We must stop the yellow fever from destroying our country!" There was a spattering of applause from the crowd.

"What's the yellow fever?" Tony asked loudly, his voice carrying to those standing around. "It sounds like a disease."

"It is a disease." A man's deep voice answered behind them. "It's a disease of yellow-skinned people coming into our country, taking our jobs and our money!"

The voice was vaguely familiar and Andrea turned around to scan the crowd. Two rows back she spotted a tall, thin man, his head towering above the crowd.

"That's Stilts," she whispered, feeling the hairs on the back of her neck begin to bristle.

"Yeah," Tony agreed. "And look!" Forgetting himself, he pointed excitedly. "Chubbs is right beside him!"

Andrea grabbed his finger and quickly pulled it down and out of sight. "Don't draw attention to us. Wherever those two are, trouble usually isn't too far behind! Turn around."

"I'll bet Mean-Eyed Max is involved in this too," Tony said, resisting the urge to search the crowd.

"I wouldn't be surprised," Vance said. "Don't you think that guy looks pretty big?" He nodded his head in the direction of one of the hooded figures walking off stage. "I'll bet that's him."

They turned their eyes back to the stage as Mr. Robertson waved to his wife. She stepped daintily to centre stage, looking like a little girl, standing beside her big husband. "The Klan is eager to have new members," she invited, her smile large and welcoming, "including you women. We have a special ladies' uniform I'm sure you'll love. I hope to see you at our offices on the corner of Ominica Street and Main."

"It's like she's inviting new neighbours to a tea party," Rosie muttered darkly.

"Sure," Vance agreed sarcastically, "as long as they're the right skin colour or nationality!" He shook his head in disgust.

"And now, in the name of our organization, we have a ritual to perform," Red Thompson announced, sounding like the master of ceremonies in a three ring circus.

The men in uniforms had moved off the stage and for a moment Andrea lost track of them. The Klan, she said silently, anxiously trying to remember where she had heard that name before.

"Look, something else is happening now!" Beanie shouted above the gasp of the crowd.

Suddenly flames rose in the sky as the large wooden cross was set on fire. Flames shot out from the wood, brilliant red and blue against the night sky.

"I don't like this," Andrea whispered, her eyes riveted to the spectacular sight.

"It looks really scary to see a cross on fire," Tony whispered, moving closer to Andrea for comfort.

Beanie sidled in close too, her huge eyes reflecting the flames.

"I think we've seen enough here," Rosie decided, flipping her notebook shut. "Let's see if we can be one of the first automobiles to leave. It's going to be hazardous driving back to town tonight."

Nodding in agreement, Vance quickly bundled up the camera and they all moved off in search of the car.

Most people were still standing frozen, watching the burning of the giant cross. A couple of the costumed figures were moving toward the cars as well. "I wonder where they're going in such a hurry?" Vance asked, quickening his pace. "I'm going to ask them what the name of this organization is. It can't just be the Klan."

They all hurried after Vance, not wanting to be left behind, although Tony lingered behind them. He wasn't sure he wanted to be too close to the faceless figures in white.

Vance had already caught up to the men and had asked his question by the time the others came within earshot. "We're Klansmen," one of the ghostly figures was saying. Tony could barely look at the man; the costume gave him the creeps.

"Our official name is the Ku Klux Klan."

"Oh!" Andrea's knees went weak and she sank to the ground. Horrified, she put her hands against her cheeks. "It's the KKK," she whispered hoarsely, her face as ghastly white as the costumes.

"You're from the newspaper," the man in the uniform stated, his hood bending closer to Vance and Rosie. He was immense, towering above them, a mountain of white, billowing material. Just looking at him gave Andrea the creeps. He sounded just like Mean-Eyed Max.

"Make sure you write the truth about us," the man continued, his voice low and threatening.

"What is the truth?" Rosie asked. Her voice shook, but she squared her shoulders, holding her head high.

"The truth is that we're just an ordinary organization of people looking to protect our country and its people," he stated.

"Yes, but by the sound of it, you're only protecting the 'chosen' people, the ones you've decided are special or privileged. You're not going to protect all people," Vance interjected. "You're not going to protect the Chinese people."

The two Klansmen closed in on Vance. He almost disappeared, lost in the yards of white material of their costumes. "We're protecting you, boy, unless you go against us. Side with us and you'll be fine. Protect the others, and you'd better watch out."

The voice was low and sinister, sending chills down Andrea's spine. "We are the Hooded Knights of the organization and our job is to protect our cause. We don't want no coolies taking our jobs, making money we should be making, marrying our women. We want them out of Canada. And don't you go getting in our way, trying to protect your coolie friends. Stay out of our way," he sneered, raising an arm and pointing at Rosie and the others all frozen with fear. "We have plans for people who don't co-operate."

Andrea and the others watched numbly as the Hooded Knights disappeared between the rows of parked cars and horse drawn buggies. "They threatened us," Tony whispered, his face ghostly white.

"That was Mean-Eyed Max," Andrea whispered. The mere mention of his name scared her.

"I've seen enough," Rosie said, her voice trembling. "Let's get out of here before something really bad happens."

"I don't think they like reporters," Vance muttered, picking up the camera again. "The way they threatened us, you'd think we were dealing with gangsters like Ol' Scarface!"

"Well Mean-Eyed Max and his men are gangsters," Andrea emphasized with a shudder.

The group of friends walked quickly to their car and climbed in. "You drive," Rosie told Vance. "I'm shaking. This group really frightens me."

"Sure thing." Vance patted her shoulder and helped Rosie into the passenger seat. He swung into the driver's seat and started the car. A few others were beginning to drive away and Vance pulled into the line of cars heading toward town. The going was slow.

Tony was sure they could have all gotten out of the car and walked faster!

From the back seat, Andrea turned and watched as the flames from the cross rose steadily into the sky. She shivered and turned away, the sight forever seared into her memory.

"The Ku Klux Klan is bad news," she told the silent occupants of the car, now that she was able to speak freely. "I didn't know they had a following in Canada. I know that they're pretty big in the United States. They're what we call a hate group in our time."

"A hate group," Beanie questioned. "What's that?"

"It's just what it sounds like," Andrea replied. "In this case it's a group of people that promote hatred of anyone who isn't white, like the Chinese and Japanese and especially the black people in the United States. They do horrible things."

"Like what?" Rosie asked turning in her seat. Like magnets, her eyes were automatically drawn to the burning cross.

Andrea thought for a moment, feeling sick to her stomach. She didn't want to say too much and scare everyone, and yet they needed to know what they were up against. "I don't know that much about the Klan, but I do know that they lynched people, especially the black people."

"Lynched?" Beanie said. "What does that mean?" She shivered, wrapping her arms around herself.

"It doesn't sound very good."

"It was horrible," Andrea agreed, remembering the few movies and documentaries she had seen on television. "If a black man did something that the Klan considered bad, or against their laws, they would hunt him down and kill him."

"They killed people because their skin was a different colour?" Beanie said. "That doesn't make any sense!"

Andrea nodded. "Can you imagine being chased through the woods or wherever, by someone wearing those outfits?"

Tony shuddered, clutching his knapsack against his chest. "It must have been terrible."

"Sometimes they chased people on horseback. The horses had costumes on too. It must have been terrifying for the ones being chased. When they caught them, and they usually did, they would tar and feather them; sometimes they would hang them. And if a black family moved into a white neighbourhood, they would terrorize the family to get them to move. They'd put on those costumes and throw rocks through the windows. They burned crosses on the front lawns and things like that."

"That's dreadful," Rosie said, shaking her head. "Why are these people in Moose Jaw? We don't want them here."

"It's cruel," Vance stated, his hands gripping the large steering wheel as the car bumped along in the rutted field. "They're no better than Ol' Scarface and Mean-Eyed Max! They're bullies using strong-arm tactics to get their own way."

Vance braked suddenly, sending everyone in the car lurching forward. "Oh!" Rosie stifled a scream as two Hooded Knights on horses rode directly in front of them. One man stayed in the yellow beam of the car's headlights making it impossible for Vance to move forward.

The other man drew his horse close to Rosie's side of the car. "Remember what we said," he yelled, leaning toward her, the gaping eyeholes leering. "We know where you live!" He laughed, an evil sound that echoed into the night, then gripped Rosie's shoulder.

"Ouch," Rosie winced, trying to pull away.

"Hey! Leave her alone," Vance yelled, reaching across Rosie to push the man away. The other mounted figure was on the driver's side of the car within seconds. He grabbed Vance's arm and began to twist as Vance fought in vain, to free himself. Andrea was sure that his arm would be broken. Reaching over the seat, she punched ineffectually at the Knight.

"What's going on here?" an authoritative voice asked. All heads whipped toward the sound. A police officer had ridden up on his horse, his billy club in hand. "Are these, uh, men bothering you?" he asked Rosie and Vance, deliberately stalling on the word "men."

"Yay!" Tony cheered softly from the back seat. "It's Officer Paterson!"

Beanie beamed. "That's my Pop!" Relief was written all over her face.

"There's no trouble at all," one of the masked men said, quickly unhanding Rosie.

"We were just giving them directions," the other added as he backed his horse away from the car. They moved quickly away, but not before turning around once more to stare at the automobile, their large, black-holed eyes glaring.

"They're trying to intimidate you," Officer Paterson said, a worried expression on his face. He stared after them as they disappeared into the crowd.

"Well, they're doing a good job of it," Rosie answered. She rubbed at her shoulder, wincing in pain. "That man had a strong grip."

"He's trying to tell us what to report in the paper," Vance told his stepfather. "They'll use force on us if we don't do what they say."

"I don't like the look of this organization," Officer Paterson commented, looking around. "I'll keep an eye on things here for a while, and then I'll swing by your place, Rosie. I'll be making a report about this at the police station too. Don't worry." He started to turn his horse around and then moved back closer to the car. "Don't worry," he repeated, leaning in closely, talking softly, "but be careful. I don't trust these people at all."

"You should nose around the old warehouse," Vance added. "That's where their office is, in the space where the laundry business was."

Officer Paterson nodded. "But you know we can't do much more than keep an eye on the warehouse unless we suspect something illegal is going on. As far as I know, no one has complained about them. This is the only incident I've had reported to me."

"What about Mr. Wong?" Tony asked from the backseat. "He was just going to report a problem a while ago."

"Is that so?" the constable rubbed his chin. "That must have happened while I was here at the rally. I'll make sure to check that out on my way home."

"Well, I wouldn't be surprised if there's more going on than meets the eye," Rosie muttered, still rubbing her shoulder. "They sure have a way of getting what they want. I'm going to be black and blue for days."

"Drive carefully, son," Officer Paterson said as he turned his horse back toward the crowd.

Andrea smiled in spite of herself. Didn't her parents say the very same thing in the present, every time she drove anywhere? Some things never changed.

The rest of the trip back into Moose Jaw was quiet and uneventful. Andrea sat huddled in the middle of the back seat, her arms wrapped around Tony and Beanie, lost in her own thoughts and worries.

The Ku Klux Klan? In Moose Jaw? Andrea could

barely believe it. She thought it was strictly a group in the United States. It was scary and disheartening to think that the Klan had existed in Canada in the 1920s.

Having taken a longer route, Vance swung around the corner onto Ominica Street, cruising slowly past the Klan office. A light shone through the window, showing a couple of wooden desks and chairs. A poster advertising the open-air meeting was propped up in the window. "Those guys are up to no good," he stated as they continued up the street to Rosie's place.

Vance parked the car and they all climbed out wearily, feeling as if they'd been gone for a thousand years. "It gives me the creeps every time I think of it," Beanie said, shivering slightly in the cool night air. "That burning cross was so scary."

"It still looks scary," Tony said, pointing to the west. There, in the distance, the cross still burned brightly, visible for miles across the prairie grasslands.

"That Klan terrifies me," Rosie said. "I don't like being threatened like that."

"Me either," they all answered, moving as one through the wooden gate and into the yard.

"But do you think they'd actually do something to hurt us?" Beanie asked.

The question was left unanswered, for suddenly the screeching tires of a car sounded, moving swiftly up the street, a couple of tough-looking men hanging out of the windows, rocks in their hands.

"Get down!" Vance yelled, pushing everyone to the ground. He threw himself face down on top of them.

Tony, who had fallen to one side of the others, crawled closer to the fence, keeping his eyes peeled on the car. He could just make out three shapes inside. The man on the passenger side wore a hat, his head tilted out the window as he scrutinized the houses. As the car careened to a stop in front of Rosie's house, his hat blew off and bounced into the street. Even in the dark, Tony could see bushy red hair and a red moustache.

"That's Red Thompson," he gasped, recognizing the man who had been on stage.

"My hat!" Thompson called as it rolled to a stop on the road. It looked like he was going to get out of the car and go after it.

"No time for that," the driver called from inside the car. It sounded like Mr. Robertson. Thompson swore loudly while the other men laughed. "Just do what we came to do."

A loud boom and the sound of shattering glass filled the air.

"Good! That ought to teach them a lesson!"

TROUBLE FOR SARAH

The automobile zoomed away as quickly as it had come, leaving the group frozen like statues on the ground. "It's clear now," Vance said, slowly rising and looking down the street. "It's safe." He reached down and helped Rosie to her feet.

The porch light blazed on and Sarah stepped gingerly through the broken glass, a horrified expression on her face. "Are you all okay?" She asked, stepping automatically to Vance's side.

Vance's arms came up and around her in a quick hug of assurance. "Yes, we're all fine. They were just trying to scare us."

"Well, they sure did," Rosie answered gruffly. She stared at the front door. The window had been knocked out and glass was strewn all over the front porch and into the hallway. "Someone wants to make sure that we write only what they want us to write. I wonder who that would be?" Her voice became sarcastic. They all knew who had broken the window in the door.

"We'll report it to the police, of course." Sarah said, surveying the mess.

"Did anyone get a look at the automobile?" Rosie asked.

They all stood by silently shaking their heads. "It was Red Thompson!" Tony reported, "And that's his hat." Racing into the street, he picked up the derby and brought it back to the group.

Rosie took it from him. Turning it over in her hands, she looked closely at it. "Some men put their initials in their hats so they don't get them mixed up, but I don't see anything written in this one."

"It looks brand new," Sarah added.

"Looks like he's hatless now," Rosie commented dryly. "It's an expensive hat. A person wouldn't likely have two of these."

"I'll get the broom and start cleaning up," Beanie offered, heading toward the steps. "Here's one of the rocks they used." She lifted it from the floor just inside the door. "Whoever threw this was really strong." She turned it over, examining it.

"Look!" Tony said excitedly. "There's a note tied to it."

A piece of crumpled white paper was fastened to

the rock with string. "Let me see it." Vance had a small pocket knife in his hand. He swiftly cut the string, pulled the note off, and opened it. "Beware," he read, squinting over the small, messy handwriting. "Quit teaching those coolies how to read and write English, if you know what's good for you."

"Oh," Sarah gasped. "That's about me!" She paled visibly, swaying into Andrea.

Rosie quickly steadied Sarah as Vance set the rock down and took her arm, leading her toward the stairs. "Don't worry," he soothed, walking behind her in case her knees gave way. "We'll report this. We'll keep you safe."

"It's not that so much," Sarah responded, her voice indignant. "It's just that I'm not doing anything wrong. In fact, I'm doing something good. What's this world coming to, when someone wants to help and they get threatened with violence!" Her voice got stronger and more indignant as she spoke.

Sarah stopped at the bottom of the steps. "My goodness!" She suddenly realized that in the frenzy of activity she hadn't even greeted her friends Andrea and Tony. Turning quickly, she opened her arms. "What a wonderful pleasure to see you two again, even in these horrid circumstances."

"Sarah," Andrea said, reaching to hug her. "I'm sorry about the rock."

"Me, too," Tony said, falling into the hug. "Don't worry, I'll help protect you, too."

Sarah smiled at the determined look on his face. "I know you will. Why, you're almost as tall as I am!" She pinched his cheek lovingly and then herded them up the stairs. "I'll make tea – it'll calm my nerves."

The wooden floor creaked as they all entered Rosie's kitchen. "I live downstairs now," Sarah said, proudly.

"But not for long," Vance pointed out, grinning. "We want to get married soon."

"Married?!" Andrea exclaimed, staring into their young faces.

"You're way too young," Tony blurted. "You're just teenagers! Nobody gets married that young in our time." Remembering the hat still clutched in his hands, he set it on the floor near Alan's bedroom door.

"Well, Vance will be twenty soon and I'm eighteen. I don't want to be an old maid," Sarah pointed out. "I'd just as soon get married and start our family."

"What's –" Tony started to ask, but Andrea nudged his arm and shook her head and he fell silent. They were way too young to get married, he thought. Why was Andrea suddenly agreeing with them?

Andrea pulled Tony aside and whispered in his ear. "They do get married, silly, remember? Sarah is our grandmother, after all."

"Oh yeah," Tony breathed, a bemused look on his face. "I forgot."

"We're just waiting for Vance to get on permanently at the newspaper office–and he will," Sarah continued, confidently, her voice glowing with pride. She glided across the room to stand beside him, leaning her head on his shoulder.

"If that's the case," Vance muttered, tossing his notebook onto the kitchen table and sitting down heavily on a wooden chair, "then why are so many of my articles rejected or sent back for rewriting?"

"I've told you, you're too emotional when you write, Vance," Rosie reminded him. "When you write for the newspaper you have to state the facts and that's it, no opinions!"

"Oh yeah," Tony suddenly remembered. "My teacher is always talking about 'the Who? What? Where? When? Why? And sometimes How?' We published a newspaper in our classroom. It was hard work. I had to write an editorial! I didn't even know what it was!"

"For some reason there are a lot of reporters vying for jobs with the newspaper right now," Rosie gently reminded Vance. "The competition is tough. Keep working at it, Vance. Don't get discouraged." She patted his shoulder. "Your writing is excellent."

"Maybe writing for the newspaper isn't the job for me," Vance sighed, his shoulders hunched. "I have been trying. I just don't seem to be getting anywhere."

Beanie came marching up the stairs, broom in hand. "Hadn't we better report the rock and the broken window to the police?"

"You're right," Vance agreed. Slipping his note-book into his pocket, he stood up. "I'll go report it and then head home to work on an article about that open-air meeting. It's been a long evening. Who has the note?"

Rosie handed it over to Vance, who folded it once and started to slip it into his notebook. His hand stalled halfway and he looked at the paper, rubbing it slightly between his fingers. "You know, this looks like the same paper that was used for Mr. Wong's note."

"Let's see it," Tony called, lunging for it. Everyone crowded around, reaching to feel the paper.

"I think you're right," Andrea agreed as she studied the handwriting.

"Oh no," Sarah whispered, her face pasty white. "You mean Mr. Wong was threatened too?"

"This is a job for the police," Vance decided, clap-ping his soft-brimmed hat on his head. "I'll take this note over. I hope Pa is still there. He'll want to see it."

"Come on, Beanie." He reached over to give Sarah a kiss and then hugged Tony and Andrea. "It's good to see you two. I'm glad you're here. It looks like we may need your help. Again!"

Beanie waved goodbye and followed Vance, shut-ting the door behind them.

Our help, Andrea thought, as a picture of her very sick grandfather suddenly filled her mind. She could-n't help them solve anything! She had to concentrate on getting that notebook and getting back to the present! Grandpa Talbot's life might depend on it!

"Vance doesn't look very happy," Andrea couldn't help noticing, as she gazed at the closed door. "Even before the rock incident. Is he all right?"

"Too many things have happened lately, and it's really gotten him down," Sarah sighed. "He isn't having as much success at the newspaper as he'd like and that's really eating away at him. You know, if he can write a good story about that meeting you all attended, that would sure boost his confidence. It's been really frustrating for him, trying to learn the business."

They drank their tea in silence, worry hanging in the air like a thick grey cloud. It was decided that Andrea would sleep on Sarah's sofa and Tony would have the extra bed in Baby Alan's room. "Sh-h-h," Rosie warned Tony as he turned to open the door, "I don't want him waking up now. I have to work on that article tonight and get it to the newspaper office as soon as I can."

"I can't wait to see him," Andrea gushed. "I'll bet he's talking!"

Rosie beamed. "A mile a minute, but it's baby chatter. I can understand most of it, but sometimes even I'm stumped."

Tony tiptoed into the dark room, pausing to look down into the crib next to the wall. Baby Alan was asleep, his rump up in the air, a thumb stuck in his mouth. Only he didn't look like a baby anymore, he looked like a sturdy toddler.

Letting his backpack drop to the floor with a quiet thump, Tony stood for a moment assessing how he felt. Fine, he decided, even though life here was in turmoil. But there were still things he had to do. he quickly checked his blood sugar and took his insulin. Undressing quietly, he fell into bed and was asleep in seconds.

Andrea had a harder time getting to sleep. The sofa was narrow and hard and the blanket kept sliding to the floor. As tired as she was, she couldn't get her mind to turn off; pictures of Grandpa, pale and sick in the hospital, haunted her. What if he died while she and Tony were stuck in the past?

Her thoughts turned to young Vance and how unhappy he was. How could she help both of them? She couldn't lose herself in this trip to the past as she had done before. There were too many things to worry about, too many things happening in the present that she needed to know. She didn't want to be in the past, wondering, she wanted to be standing beside Grandpa, holding his hand, telling him everything would be okay.

The only thing she knew for sure was that she had to get Vance's notebook. That was what Grandpa wanted. But how was she going to get it from Vance?

He seemed to carry it with him everywhere he went. She wondered if she dared ask him about it. And how would she know if it was the right notebook?

The questions swirled in her brain like an out-of-control merry-go-round, as the moon advanced across the sky. She watched as the pale light played hide-and-seek with the thin curtains veiling the window. Finally, as the sky began to lighten in the east, she fell into a restless, exhausted sleep.

WHAT WILL ANDREA WEAR?

The sounds of people walking overhead jerked Andrea to awareness and she sat up abruptly. Her eyes took in the neat and tidy living area, the small wooden table and two chairs across the narrow room. Where was she? The sun shone brightly in through the window as a gentle breeze stirred the crisp white curtains. A framed picture of Vance and Sarah sat on the top of a bookshelf at the end of the sofa.

"Oh," she remembered. She was back in time.

The door opened quietly and Beanie stuck her head inside. "Good morning," she called when she spied Andrea sitting up. "I was sent to tell you that breakfast is being served upstairs at Rosie's. Are you coming?"

Andrea nodded, stretching tiredly. "I'll be right up," she promised.

Beanie shut the door and headed back upstairs while Andrea quickly got dressed, pulling her moose sweatshirt over her head. Finger-combing her hair, she splashed water on her face and then headed upstairs.

Noisy confusion greeted her as soon as she pushed open the door. Tony was helping Beanie set the table. Sarah and Rosie were cooking breakfast, and Vance was tossing Alan into the air and catching him. High-pitched squeals of delight filled the room.

"Good morning," Andrea called over the din. Baby Alan chortled and then demanded to be put down. Once on the floor, he tottered over to Andrea and stood staring solemnly up at her, his head tilted to one side.

"He doesn't recognize you," Tony said from across the room. He put the plates on the table and slid across the floor on sock feet to stand beside Alan. "He didn't recognize me at first, either, but now he's used to me, aren't you, boy?" Reaching down, he ruffled the child's fine curls.

Alan lifted his arms to Tony, who picked him up. "It's okay," Tony told him, reassuring the child. "That's Andrea."

Nestled in Tony's arms, Alan felt braver. Reaching out with a chubby finger, he touched the front of Andrea's sweatshirt, running chubby fingers over the embroidered moose. "Moo," he said, imitating a cow.

Tony laughed. "He thinks you're a cow!"

"Thanks," Andrea said, her expression pained.

"That's a moose," Tony said, pointing to the antlers.

"Moo," Alan repeated. He raised his eyes to Andrea. "Moo," he said. Grinning, he tried to throw himself out of Tony's arms, grabbing at the moose with both fists.

"See, he likes you," Tony smiled.

"He likes the moose," Andrea corrected. She caught Alan up in her arms and kissed the top of his head.

Turning toward Vance, Andrea suddenly remembered. "What did the police say?"

Frowning and shaking his head, he sighed. "They were very surprised. I guess no one's reported this kind of thing before. They promised to keep a closer eye on this house and the street, and we're to report anything else unusual to them immediately."

"And the paper the note was written on? Was it the same?"

Vance shrugged. "I told Pa about it, since the other constables didn't seem all that interested in it. He'll check into it and get back to us."

"Breakfast is ready," Rosie announced, and everyone took a seat around the table. "Scrambled eggs, toast, and fried potatoes."

Andrea watched as Tony dug into the food with gusto. She wondered if she needed to worry about him taking his insulin. His eyes met hers over the table and he nodded as he took a big bite of crispy toast. "I took care of it," he mouthed.

Andrea smiled and nodded. She was glad Tony was taking more responsibility for his diabetes. Maybe he was growing up.

"Where's the morning paper?" Rosie asked between bites of breakfast. "Did our articles about the rally make the front page?"

Scowling, Vance thumped the paper on the table. "Your article did, as usual. Mine was rejected. Again."

Sarah patted his hand in sympathy. "It's okay, Vance. You've only been at this for a short time. You'll catch on."

"I'm not sure I'm cut out to be a newspaper reporter." Jumping to his feet, the chair scraping against the wooden floor, Vance stalked across the room. "I'll see you later." He threw the door open so hard it banged against the wall and then bounced back, slamming shut after him.

Alan stared at the door. His lower lip quivered, then he burst into tears, his piercing cries echoing around room. "That's how I feel," Sarah said, blinking back tears of her own. Reaching for Alan, she comforted him in her arms, her lips pressed against his cheek. "Sh-h-h," she murmured.

"Poor Vance," Andrea said, feeling sorry for him. "Why don't they like his stories?"

"He's the new guy, so he isn't very experienced yet," Beanie said.

"And it sure doesn't help that my articles get published," Rosie sighed. "I think he feels he has to compete against me. I've been doing this for a few years now and he's just beginning."

Tony rattled the newspaper, rapidly turning the pages. "Hey! Look!" he pointed excitedly to a small column on the third page. "Vance did too get published! This is the article he must have written last night about the rock going through the window!" He paused for a minute, rapidly reading it. "It's good," he decided, smiling. "It gives all the necessary information."

Rosie leaned over his shoulder too, reading. "It's short and sweet and exactly what the editors are looking for. I just hope he can learn to write consistently."

Sarah rolled her eyes and sighed. "Vance does try my patience at times. He didn't even look for this article in the paper!"

Andrea pushed her chair back from the table. "I'm going to go find Vance and tell him about this. Maybe he'll feel better." She reached for the paper, tucking it under her arm. "Where do you think I'll find him?"

Beanie thought for a minute then jumped up. "Come on," she said. "I'll show you where he might be." They hurried to the door.

Sarah looked disapprovingly at Andrea's clothes.

"You'd better change first. Young women in this era don't go around dressed in pants, especially not dungarees like you're wearing."

"Dunga-what?!" Tony exclaimed, shaking his head.

"She means jeans," Andrea interpreted, looking down at her slim hip-huggers. "Well, I have nothing else to wear."

"I wish I could wear clothes like that," Beanie sighed, looking in disgust at her own prim-and-proper dress, another variation of the style she'd worn yesterday.

"Come on," Sarah said, taking her by the hand. "I have just the dress for you." She led Andrea back downstairs and into her small living area. "Wait right here," she said, disappearing into her bedroom.

Andrea heard the scraping sound of hangers being pushed across a wooden rod and then Sarah returned. "Here it is. What do you think?" she asked eagerly as she held a dress up for inspection.

It was navy blue and long. Andrea was sure it would hang several centimetres below her knee. "It looks all right," she murmured, her eyes skittering away from Sarah's. She didn't want to hurt her feelings, but the dress was old-fashioned and ugly. She was glad none of her friends would ever see her in it. "I'll go try it on," she mumbled, trying to muster some enthusiasm.

"Use the bedroom," Sarah said, grandly waving her arm toward the door. "I have a looking glass in there so you can see yourself."

Looking glass? It took Andrea a moment to realize Sarah was talking about a mirror. She went into the bedroom, pulling off her sweatshirt as she went. Too bad jeans weren't the fad, she thought ruefully, because they sure were comfortable.

Reluctantly, she pulled the dress over her head, poking her arms out of the short sleeves. She was right; the hem fell below her knees. A large white collar lay across her shoulders, making her face look more pale and angular than usual. It was a straight-line dress with a dropped waistline that made her look as thin and shapeless as a pencil. "I don't think I should wear this dress, Sarah," Andrea said as she entered the room. "It doesn't suit me, it's not my style."

Eyeing her critically, Sarah motioned for Andrea to turn around. Biting her lips, she softly agreed. "I think it looks better on me."

"I look like a twig," Andrea smoothed the dress down the front and sighed, wishing the dress looked more flattering on her.

"We have to go." Beanie's head suddenly appeared in the doorway. "Vance won't stay there all day."

"Just wear it," Sarah said. "You look fine."

Shrugging, Andrea returned to the bedroom, coming back in her thick-soled running shoes. "I only have these to wear."

Beanie giggled. "You look a spectacle."

"I don't think my shoes would fit you," Sarah said, inspecting Andrea's much larger feet.

Sighing, Andrea headed for the door. "Never mind," she said. "At least I'll be able to run, if I need to."

"I'm the one who'll need to be able to run," Sarah retorted.

"What?" Andrea stopped and turned around. "Why?"

Squaring her shoulders, Sarah looked Andrea straight in the eye. "Today is one of the days I go to Wong's Café to tutor, and no rock or threatening note is going to keep me away."

THE DARE

"Don't worry," Beanie spoke up. "I already figured Sarah would want to tutor today, so I asked Tony to escort her down Main Street. He was really excited to go with her."

"What about Alan?" Andrea suddenly remembered.

"Oh, Rosie and I take turns with him. She'll stay home for a few hours until I get back and then she'll check in at the newspaper office," Sarah reported. "Now go, so I can get ready. And be gentle with Vance," she said softly. "I'm worried about him." Beanie and Andrea nodded and left the room.

The warm sun greeted the girls as they pushed the front door open, its empty frame gaping and sinister-looking, somehow. A shard of glass about the size of a fist was still wedged into the right-hand bottom corner. It reminded them of the rock and the awful note and they hurried past.

Andrea was concerned about how much time everything seemed to be taking. She just wanted to get back to the present, notebook in hand, and make sure Grandpa was all right.

Lost in their own thoughts, they quietly crossed Main, but not before Andrea had inspected the Klan office. A small group of people were gathering there already. "I hope they're not joining the organization," she whispered as they started across the street.

"Me too," Beanie shuddered, staring darkly at a young man about Vance's age. "I don't think they really understand what it's all about."

They crossed the street in silence. "Where are we going?" Andrea asked.

"To Crescent Park, of course. Vance has a special place there where he likes to write."

Beanie led the way through the park and down the embankment to the creek. She easily jumped it and started up the other side. "Just a minute," Andrea called. Stretching her leg, she tried to leap across, but the dress impeded her progress. Her foot just missed the bank on the other side of the creek and she landed with a resounding splash in the water.

Whirling around to see what had happened, Beanie burst out laughing.

"It's not funny," Andrea said sternly, trying not to smile. She was standing calf-deep in the water, her running shoes sticking in the mud on the bottom of the creek bed.

"What happened?" Beanie asked between giggles. Quickly sliding down the bank, she grasped Andrea's hand to pull her out of the water.

"I forgot I was wearing this dress," Andrea said, looking down at it with scorn. "I didn't realize until I'd actually jumped that my legs wouldn't stretch far enough to get across the water." She laughed. "I'd have had to hike it up to my waist to make it across."

Beanie's eyes grew owlishly large. "That wouldn't have been a good idea."

"Of course not," Andrea retorted. Carefully, she moved her feet, trying to keep her balance on the uneven creek bottom. They made squishing sounds, muddy water bubbling up around her ankles. "I hate wet feet," she muttered.

Suddenly she remembered landing in the puddle at the hospital. A picture of the rainstorm flooded into her mind and she saw Grandpa Vance lying sick in the hospital. All her worries rushed back to her like a one-ton brick landing on her shoulders. "Show me where Vance is," she said grimly. "We need to hurry."

Noticing the change in Andrea, Beanie rushed across the park toward a natural gully. It was about halfway through the park and could be reached by walking behind the library. The trees were larger here, the banks of the creek steeper, with some large, flat rocks just perfect for sitting. "Vance is usually in this gully somewhere. He likes to write here."

Andrea could see why. The steep banks made a natural and private ravine. With the area almost completely covered in shrubs and bushes, a person could sit there all day hidden from the rest of the world. She realized with a start that this location was right beside where the amphitheatre sat in modern day Moose Jaw, just behind the library in Crescent Park.

"Does Vance do much writing?" she asked, wondering how to ask about the notebook without raising any suspicions.

But Beanie seemed eager to talk. "He writes a lot of stories, his newspaper articles, and even poetry."

"Does he do it all in that little notebook?"

"That's his notebook for work," Beanie answered, carefully choosing her steps as she worked her way down the side of the gully. "He has a nice leather-bound book that he uses for his stories and poetry."

"That's probably what Grandpa wants!" Andrea burst out as she slid down the bank after Beanie.

"What did you say?" Beanie asked from below.

"Oh, uh-h," Andrea hedged, wishing she hadn't talked out loud. "I was just – uh-h, just wondering if Vance would read something to me; something he's written." How clever, coming up with that idea, she thought. If Vance read her something, he would have to show her the notebook. She might even be able to get it from him on the pretext of wanting to read his work.

"What are you doing down here?" a harsh voice called and the girls jumped. "I don't like to be interrupted when I'm writing." He glared at Beanie. "You know that."

"We're just worried about you, Vance," Andrea said pulling out the newspaper. "And we wanted to show you this. Look!" she said, excitedly pointing at the paper as she shook it in his face. "You did so get published, see?"

Vance looked. A slight smile played on his lips as he scanned it. "I made it," he said. "At least it's something, even if it's small."

"Well, you have to start somewhere," Andrea reminded him, shaking her head at his grouchy mood, "and it's not usually at the top. Most people have to work their way up, you know!" He really should be happy he had something published!

"Our ma is always telling Vance that, but he doesn't listen."

Andrea cleared her throat nervously. "Uh-h-h, listen, Vance, Beanie said you've written a lot of short stories and poems. I'd really like to read some. Do you think I could?" She held her breath awaiting his reply. What would she do if he said no?

"I haven't shared that part of my writing with too many people yet," Vance hedged, looking uncomfortable. His foot tapped out a fast rhythm on the rock as he raked a hand through his hair in the anxious gesture Andrea remembered so well.

"But I'm your granddaughter," Andrea blurted, desperate to get hold of the notebook.

The two stood facing one another, hands on hips, noses almost pressed together. Tension filled the air, radiating between them. Neither noticed as Beanie slipped silently away, back up the hill.

Frowning, Vance pursed his lips together, tapping his index finger against them as he mulled over her suggestion. "You know," he finally said, his words slow and thoughtful. "I might just let you read something, if you do me a favour."

Andrea felt her heart leap for joy. This was going to be much much easier than she had anticipated. "Anything," she promised, her voice light and cheerful, "as long as I get to read your work."

"Anything?" he repeated, his voice calculating. A strange light came into his eyes.

"Just name it and I'll do it," Andrea vowed. She could feel the notebook in her hands; it was just a matter of time.

"All right," Vance said. "I need some help with a story I'm working on and I know I can count on you to help me do some research." He slipped his hands into his pockets and leaned back to look Andrea straight in the eye. He pulled out a ten-dollar bill and thrust it toward her.

"Here's the money. I want you to join the Ku Klux Klan."

TONY AND BEANIE
MAKE A PLAN

Hurrying back through the park, Beanie easily jumped the creek, giggling to herself as she landed safely on the other side. How absurd Andrea had looked, stuck in the muddy creek bottom, her feet soaking. Her mind quickly moved on to more pressing issues. She had a sudden idea of something she and Tony could do. If she hurried, she would be able to catch him before he walked Sarah to Wong's Café.

Sprinting toward Main Street in a most unladylike fashion, Beanie headed toward Rosie's place, her chest heaving. She slowed to a fast walk as she sped by the Klan office. It was a hive of business. Groups of people stood near the front doors on Main, while workers unloaded trucks into the large side door off Ominica Street.

Hurrying past, Beanie arrived at Rosie's place in record time. Her throat felt as parched as the prairie grass, and it hurt. "Water," she croaked as she half fell into the kitchen at the top of the wooden stairs. "I need water."

"What's wrong with you?" Tony demanded, suspicious of Beanie's behavior.

Beanie flopped dramatically into the nearest chair. "I just ran all the way from the park. I have a plan for us, but first I need a drink!"

Tony's eyes lit up and he quickly got a glass of water. It slopped over the edges of the glass as he raced across the kitchen. "Here!" He thrust it into her hand. "What's the plan?"

"I'm sure Rosie and Vance will want inside information about that new group, the Klan, so they can write about it for the newspaper," Beanie said. "We're going to snoop around to see what we can find out." Looking around she asked, "Where is everyone?"

Tony made a face. "Rosie didn't want me to walk Sarah by myself, because of the trouble last night. She thought it'd be better if she and Baby Alan went. I was going to go too, but somehow I thought you might be back soon!" He grinned. "I'm really glad I waited. I'll have much more fun with you!"

"I know," Beanie agreed, picking up her water glass.

"I was watching for you out of the window in Baby

Alan's room," Tony told her. "Did you know you can see all the way down to Main Street from here?" Beanie nodded. "You can see that warehouse plain as day. They have three trucks parked there, full of boxes. It's probably those scary ghost costumes they wear, and stuff like that."

"They're still unloading. Let's go see if we can get hired!" Beanie jumped out of her chair and raced for the door.

Tony grabbed her arm and pulled her to a stop. "They're sure not going to hire a girl!"

"Oh yeah," Beanie looked down at her rumpled dress with distain. "Why did I have to be born a girl?" She flounced back across the room and flung herself back into the chair. "Now what am I going to do?"

"Well, you could disguise yourself as a boy, just like Andrea used to do!" Tony grinned.

Beanie's eyes lit up and she sprang out of the chair throwing her arms around Tony. "You're the best great-nephew a person ever had!"

"But where are you going to find clothes?" Tony asked. "Vance's would be way too big on you."

"That's the easy part." Beanie marched to Alan's bedroom and flung open the door. "Rosie was helping collect clothes and things for a family in town. Their house burned down two weeks ago. I'll bet there's something I can wear in all the boxes under Baby Alan's bed."

They dropped to their knees, each pulling a wooden crate out from under the bed, and began pulling neatly folded clothes out and piling them on the floor.

"These look promising," Beanie said, after a while, holding a pair of faded overalls and an old plaid shirt against her body. "Go back to the kitchen," she ordered, "and I'll try these things on."

Tony did as he was directed, pulling the door closed behind him. He paced around the deserted room a few times, impatient to get going.

"I hope everyone's okay," Tony called out, thinking about Sarah and Rosie, and the threats from the Klansmen. "Maybe Sarah really should forget about tutoring for a while."

"Can you see Sarah not helping someone?" Beanie called back, her voice muffled.

"No, I guess not." Tony turned at the sound of the door opening. "I just hope they stay safe."

Beanie pursed her lips together in a thin line. "Me too," she agreed quietly. "Those Klansmen are really nasty, but it's broad daylight. Sarah and Rosie should be fine." She pirouetted around the room. "Well, how do I look?"

"You look great! I wouldn't have known it was you, Beanie." She had on the old flannel shirt and faded overalls patched on one knee. Her hair was pulled back and tucked up underneath a navy soft-brimmed hat.

"The name's Bob," she corrected. "Come on, let's go."

"Bob?" Tony questioned and then he got it. "Oh, Bob," he agreed, nodding and grinning. "I like that name for you."

Hurrying across the kitchen floor, they raced down the stairs, out of the house, into the warm sunshine.

They could see the trucks still parked at the warehouse. Its wide doors stood open and Stilts trudged back and forth carrying wooden boxes inside. He grumbled under his breath as he lifted the boxes up, sweat running down his forehead.

It was easy as pie to get a job. Stilts stood mopping a large white hanky over his forehead as they approached. "You two looking for work?" he asked.

Beanie nodded eagerly as Tony answered for them. "We sure are."

Stilts looked them up and down for a minute and Beanie held her breath, hoping he wouldn't figure out she was a girl. "Help carry those crates inside," he finally ordered, pointing into the warehouse. "I'll square with you once the job is done."

Eagerly, they each grabbed a box from the truck and carried it into the warehouse. "That was Stilts," Tony whispered as they got out of earshot and into the cool interior of the dark building. "I would've recognized him anywhere."

Beanie nodded. "Me too."

"I'm just worried he'll recognize us from last night. Keep that hat on your head."

Most of the boxes were light and easily carried. "Put those boxes in the office over there," a man called into the dimness. He waved an arm toward the open office door, his protruding stomach falling over his belt.

Beanie peered at him. "Chubbs," she announced in a quiet voice and Tony nodded.

"Where those two are, trouble usually isn't too far behind. I wonder if they had anything to do with the broken window at Rosie's house. I didn't recognize them in the car, though, but I'd know that red-haired man anywhere." Tony placed his box on the floor in the room. As he waited for Beanie to do the same, he looked around.

"This is the same office that they held Andrea in when she was kidnapped, remember?" He shuddered as scary memories flooded his mind.

"I know," Beanie said, rubbing her arms to keep the chills of fear away. She tiptoed closer to the desk, trying to get a look at some of the papers strewn across the top of it.

Tony pulled at her arm, drawing her back. "Come on, Chubbs is staring this way. We have to keep working hard or they'll fire us. Maybe we'll get a chance to look around later." They hurried outside, dodging around other workers carrying boxes.

Chubbs seemed to know the contents of every box, for he directed them to different places as they came into the warehouse. Some of the boxes went into the office, others were stacked against the far back wall of the warehouse, and still others were piled near the door to the stairs, which led down to where the underground laundry business had been in operation last year. Tony was very curious about the contents, but resisted the urge to look inside. He didn't want to draw any unwanted attention to himself or Beanie.

After an hour, Beanie and Tony were hot and sweaty, their hands grimy and bruised from the wooden crates. Tony had several small slivers in his fingers from a splintered box. They had finished unloading the lighter boxes and now carried heavier ones further into the far corners of the dark warehouse.

"What do you think is in these boxes?" Tony asked, curiosity getting the better of him.

Beanie grunted as she set her crate down. "I don't know, but whatever it is, it's heavy." She flopped down on the box. "Let's rest for a while. It's cooler in here than outside and there's not much left anyway."

Sighing, Tony sat down beside her. "I'm going to have a look inside," he said, leaning over the nearest box. Glancing around, he pried the lid off and peered inside. "Uniforms," he announced, "lots of them. It looks like they're hoping to enroll the whole town in the KKK! Who'd be stupid enough to join that organization?!"

"What about those boxes in the office?" Beanie asked. "I wonder what's in them?" She scanned the area; no one was coming. "This is the chance we've been waiting for. Let's go back to the office again and have a good look around."

Moving cautiously across the floor, they kept their eyes peeled. "I hope you're right about this," Tony murmured as they hurried across the floor. "I don't want to be caught in here."

"You stay out here and act as a lookout," Beanie said, motioning for him to stand beside the door. "Call out if you see or hear anything."

Nodding, Tony tried to keep one eye trained on the warehouse door, while he followed Beanie's movements in the office, too. She walked rapidly to the desk and shuffled through the papers. "Most of this paper looks like flyers." A box was open beside the desk. "That's what we carried in in those heavy boxes. Flyers advertising the Ku Klux Klan, and asking people to buy memberships." She stuffed a piece of paper into the breast pocket of her overalls.

Her eyes passing swiftly over the room, Beanie noticed that the stack of boxes they had piled up wasn't flush against the wall. "This can't all be flyers," she muttered. "I wonder what else is in there?"

Suddenly Stilts's voice boomed into the warehouse. "I thought we had two more kids. Where are they?" Both Beanie and Tony jumped sky high.

"Hide!" Tony called, waving frantically at her from the doorway. "I'll try to hold them off!"

He sprinted across the warehouse floor, not sure what his plan was. A hand clamped itself on his shoulder and pulled him up short. "W-were you looking for me?" Tony stuttered.

"Where have you been?" Chubbs demanded suspiciously. His eyes narrowing as he looked Tony up and down. "Where's your friend?"

"Uh-h," Tony tried to kick his brain into gear. "Sh-he, he had to go. I said I'd collect the money we earned." He pulled his shoulders up, trying to keep the quiver of fear out of his voice.

"Oh you did, did you?" Chubbs took a threatening step toward Tony, his fist raised.

"Leave the kid alone," Stilts ordered, thumping Chubbs on the back. "We've got more important things to worry about than him. Just pay him and let's get back to work. I'm going to the office."

Oh no, Beanie thought, her heart jumping in her throat. They're heading this way! Eyes wildly scanning the small room, she searched frantically for a place to hide! Spying the tall stack of boxes in front of the wall, she dove behind it just as Stilts entered the room.

"Now beat it, kid," she heard Chubbs growl, then heard the steady clump of his shoes on the warehouse floor. "I got rid of him, but I don't trust him. There's something familiar about him, but I don't know what. I still think that other kid's around here somewhere."

Beanie heard the scrape of a chair as one of the men sat down. "Why would a kid want to hang around? There's nothing here," said Stilts.

"No?" Chubbs questioned as a drawer scraped open. "Just *this,*" he said.

Very curious, Beanie slid as quietly as she could to the edge of the boxes and peered out. Stilts sat at the desk with Chubbs standing slightly behind him. Both men had their backs to the boxes. There was the clunk of something heavy being put on the desk.

"Where's the key?" Chubbs asked.

Stilts reached into his pocket, pulling a huge ring of keys out. "It's one of these. Anyway, we were ordered not to touch that money box. It's none of our business how much money's in there."

"Aw-w-w," Chubbs complained, making a grab for the keys. "I just want to see it. Feel how heavy this box is! There must be thousands of dollars there."

"Oh, yeah," Stilts agreed, his voice sounding dreamy and far away, "thousands."

"They'd never miss a bit, ya know." He rubbed his hands together. "Suppose it just happened to disappear?"

"What!?" Stilts tried to sound shocked, but Beanie could tell that he liked the idea. "Go close the door," he ordered as he grabbed the keys back. There was a rattling sound of metal on metal as he fiddled with the lock.

Reaching in, Stilts grabbed a handful of paper money and crammed it into his pants pocket. Chubbs did the same, but his fist was larger and his pocket bulged noticeably. "Not so much," Stilts complained, but Chubbs ignored him. Together they fastened the lock back into place and hid the box again. "Come on, let's get outta here. I don't want to be caught with the loot."

The door sprang open. "Well, well," a hoarse voice rasped. "What do we have here?" There was a sinister chuckle as the door clicked shut again and Mean-Eyed Max came into view. He was bigger and taller than Beanie remembered, almost a giant from her vantage point near the floor. He had to duck his head to avoid the light dangling from the ceiling.

Chubbs and Stilts cowered against the desk, stuttering and stammering so badly that Beanie almost felt sorry for them. "What are you two up to?" Mean-Eyed Max growled; then he spied the cash box. He grabbed it from them.

"Never mind. This is what I came for. Those Klansmen think they can pull the wool over my eyes. They've been holding out on paying us for our help. I'll just hold onto this little box for a while." He laughed, a sinister chuckle that sent chills running up Beanie's back.

The door clicked open again and Mean-Eyed Max strode out into the dark warehouse, his boots thudding loudly on the floor. "Come on, you two," he ordered. "Let's go. We'll take the tunnels; that way we won't be seen. They'll just think the money evaporated." He laughed harshly. It echoed through the large building in a haunting way which left goosebumps on Beanie's arms.

"Whew," both Chubbs and Stilts gasped. It sounded as if they'd been holding their breath for a long, long time.

"I thought we were dead ducks," Chubbs said.

"Me too," Stilts agreed, whirling around and pushing Chubbs toward the door. "Now let's get out of here before he gets mad."

Beanie shuffled back out of sight. Her foot knocked against the crates with a loud thump.

"Hey, did you hear that?" Chubbs whispered.

Beanie cowered behind the boxes, her breath caught in her throat as she listened to the sound of footsteps coming toward her.

GOING UNDERCOVER

Andrea joined in the long line on Main Street as she waited for her turn to register as a member of the Ku Klux Klan. People were queued up to join the group; she couldn't believe it! She hummed to herself, counted the fluffly clouds in the sky, read every sign in sight – anything to distract herself. She would not, could not think about what she was about to do.

She filled her mind with thoughts of Grandpa. How was he doing? Was he still alive? He must be, she thought. Surely she would be able to feel it if he had died. I'm doing this all for him, she chanted in her mind, as the line moved slowly, bringing her ever closer to becoming a member of that terrible group.

It wasn't like she actually believed anything the KKK espoused, Andrea reminded herself. She was merely going undercover to get information for Vance so he could write newspaper articles exposing the true nature of the Klan. Still, standing in line for all the world to see, made her feel as if she was doing something wrong. She hoped no one she knew would pass by and see her; it looked like she was supporting the KKK!

Surrounded as she was by many other people, Andrea couldn't help but eavesdrop on them. A tall, thin man in a big cowboy hat and dirty overalls stood just in front of her, in deep conversation with the man in line ahead of him. "We need an organization like this," the tall man was saying. "I'm just an honest, hardworking farmhand trying to make a decent livin' for me and my family."

A friendly-looking young couple stood behind Andrea. They looked to be Vance's age. The girl smiled at Andrea. "My name's Maria," she babbled happily, her excitement almost contagious. "This is Tymko, my husband." She stopped and smiled up affectionately at him. "Are you joining this group too? It sounds so exciting. I want to be part of something that's going to help us be a better country."

Biting her tongue, Andrea shrugged her shoulders noncommittally. She wanted to scream and shout that this wasn't the group to join. Hoping she didn't look encouraging or supportive, she turned her attention back to the men's conversation.

"Now those garlic eaters are settlin' in my area," the farmhand complained, his voice growing more animated. "They're willin' to work for peanuts and they're puttin' me outta work!"

The young girl leaned forward. "What's he talking about? Garlic eaters? Why, that's an insult!"

"Yeah, garlic eaters," the man continued, looking over his shoulder at the couple. "We don't want anymore garlic eaters and their strange ways settling in our area."

Maria drew herself up and stood rigidly beside the young man, her eyes narrowed. "You mean the Ukrainians?" Her voice was deadly calm, but Andrea could hear barely suppressed anger.

"Ukrainians, Hungarians, Russians – you name it – we don't want 'em here!"

Turning to her husband, Maria took his hand. "We're Ukrainian," she said proudly. "We're Tymko and Maria Hyshka. We're obviously in the wrong place. We don't want to have any part of a discriminating group like this!" She looked pointedly at Andrea for a moment – as if to say, what are you doing? – and then turned on her heel and walked away, taking Tymko with her.

Feeling like scum, Andrea wished she could follow along. She didn't want Maria and Tymko thinking badly of her. She didn't want them believing that she really wanted to be part of an organization that discriminated against people!

The line moved again and Andrea found herself in front of the long plate glass windows of the storefront where signs announced the membership meetings and registration times for the week. Inside the display window, she saw flyers advertising the Klan and telling in veiled language what it stood for. The costumes were also on display.

I can't do this, Andrea thought, her eyes filling with tears. How could she join such a horrible group, even if she was doing it for Vance? She wanted nothing more than to run like a frightened prairie chicken, as far away from this lineup as possible. But something held her there, rooted in line. The sun beat down upon her, making her light-headed, or was that just the worry and turmoil gnawing at her stomach? What was it that made her stay?

She blinked back the tears, waiting impatiently as time seemed to pass at a snail's pace. She watched a horse and buggy trot down the street. A couple of young women ambled by, talking excitedly, one pushing a pram. Would they get sucked into this hate group as well?

Suddenly realization snapped into her mind like a light blinking on. It was the truth that made her stay. Vance wanted to expose this group for what it was, and he needed her help to do it. Andrea determined not to let him down. She wanted the truth to come out too.

Finally the line moved again and Andrea found herself second from the door. It was taking so long! What did they talk about in there? The ten-dollar bill was clenched in her hand, her moist fingers cramped around it.

The door opened and a couple of people walked out, the heavy white Klan costumes draped over their arms. The man with the bushy red moustache and red hair motioned for Andrea to enter. Red Thompson, she realized, and stared, wondering if he knew where his hat was. Taking a deep, shaky breath, she blanked all thought out of her mind and stepped forward.

It was cool inside, a welcome reprieve from the heat of the afternoon sun. A fan turned lazily from the ceiling, pushing air around the room. "So, you want to join our organization," a familiar voice chirped and Andrea found herself face to face with Esther, the only woman onstage at the rally. She grinned eagerly at Andrea and took her arm. "Our first young woman! Welcome! I'm going to personally take care of you."

"Wait a minute," Mr. Robertson warned his wife, "we do need to ask her a few questions to determine if she is right for our organization. We don't just let anyone join." He stared hard at Andrea, through his thick glasses, as if he was trying to see inside her skin. "Are you Jewish?" he asked.

What?! Andrea thought indignantly. Why did that matter? What if she were Jewish? Struggling to keep her disgust invisible, she shook her head. "No."

"Catholic?" Mr. Robertson continued.

Outraged, Andrea wanted to turn around and march out of the room. Clenching her fists, she pushed her emotions aside. "N-no," she sputtered, staring at his collar. It was done up tightly, the rolls of his fat neck hanging over the edges. His hand came up and fingers tugged at the tight collar. Good, I hope it chokes him, she thought.

"I can see that you're not Chinese," he laughed merrily, as if he was saying something very clever. "It looks like you pass the test."

"Would it matter if she was Catholic or Jewish or Chinese?" a voice asked from behind.

Andrea turned to see a well-dressed couple standing behind her. "Just what is your mission here?" the man asked, his bushy eyebrows furled. His left hand gripped an expensive looking walking stick. "I thought this was a responsible social group, something that would be good for Moose Jaw. I'm having second thoughts about joining this organization. It sounds like it will separate and classify people, not unite them."

Red Thompson appeared out of nowhere and tried to smooth things over. Taking the man's arm, he escorted him to a desk in the corner of the room. "You look like an educated man," he was saying, his loud voice carrying.

"And rich," Mrs. Robertson added, smiling sweetly at Andrea. "Money is important, you know. Now let's see about paying your membership. You do have the money, don't you?"

Andrea handed the crumpled bill over, bile rising in her throat. The last thing she wanted to do was throw good money away on a sick organization like this.

"Oh good," Mrs. Robertson clasped her hands together and then plucked the money out of Andrea's fingers. "Fill out this membership card over by the wall," she said, indicating an empty table across the room. She eyed Andrea as if measuring her. "I'll go get you a uniform."

Taking a deep breath, Andrea took the hateful card out of Mrs. Robertson's hand and proceeded across the room. She noticed with satisfaction that Red and the well-dressed couple were in a heated debate. The man thumped his walking stick on the floor several times as if making a point.

"What is your name, dear?" Mrs. Robertson called out.

Without even thinking about it, Andrea replied, "Doreen," giving her middle name. "Doreen, uh-h, Smith."

"You can call me Esther," the woman chirped again and Andrea thought she would be sick.

Without an ounce of conscience, Andrea filled in the card, lying on every space. She gave her new false name; her cousin's address in Moose Jaw – one she knew wouldn't even exist for another sixty years. She had a feeling that Mrs. Robertson and company didn't know the town well and wouldn't even check up on that. By the look of things, they were just interested in getting their hands on the membership fees.

"Here you go, dear." Esther handed Andrea the loathsome uniform, informing her when the next meetings would be held.

Wanting to throw it on the ground and stomp on it, Andrea held the outfit loosely in one hand, almost as if she was afraid some of the hate would rub off on her. She didn't even listen to Esther talk about meetings. She wasn't planning on attending another one. Breathing a long sigh of relief, she headed for the door.

A loud crash was heard and Andrea whirled around to see Red Thompson leaning across the desk, his face almost as red as his hair. "I'll do everything in my power to shut you down!" the well-dressed man shouted, waving his cane in the air. His wife looked as if she might faint. "This group is a detriment to the unity and security of our fair town and this country!"

"Get out!" Red ordered, his fists pounding on the desk. "We don't want your kind here."

Mr. Robertson grabbed the man roughly by the arm and pulled him toward the door while his wife cowered from behind. "You heard the boss! Get out!"

Ted Rogers magically appeared and took over. "Easy," he warned Mr. Robertson. "We don't want any trouble from the police." He brushed the man off and marched the couple to the door. "Good day."

Andrea slipped out of the door behind the couple, the awful outfit still in her hands. She watched as the man took his wife's arm. "I'm certainly glad we found out what that was all about before we joined," he huffed. "I don't want any part of that group."

"Neither do I," she agreed.

Me either, Andrea thought, trying not to think too much about what she had done, or what she was carrying. Oh well, it was for a good cause, she reminded herself. Now she had lots of information she could share with Vance about the Klan. Besides, she thought, with a small grin, no one would ever have to know. This made her feel better. It would always be her and Vance's secret.

She had taken two steps down the street when a familiar voice sounded in her ear. A hand grabbed her arm and whirled her around. "Just what do you think you're doing, young lady?"

"If You Want to See Your Friend Again..."

Thinking quickly, Beanie reached into her pocket and tossed a penny across the room. The coin plunked on the floor and then circled back toward her hiding place behind the boxes. Oh no, she thought in panic as she dived behind the boxes. My diversion failed!

"What was that?!" Stilts said. He froze in his tracks quickly searching the floor.

"Are you two coming or what?" Mean-Eyed Max snarled. "I ain't got all day!"

"B-but," Chubbs sputtered, pointing toward the pile of boxes. "We heard something."

"It was a rat," Mean-Eyed Max stated. "Now get moving."

"Yes, sir." The two thugs almost tripped over themselves following their boss out of the office.

Beanie breathed a huge sigh of relief and relaxed, thanking her lucky stars–or penny–that she hadn't been spotted. She wondered briefly what they would have done with her, then pushed that scary thought away. It was better not to know those kinds of things!

Tony slipped silently into the office, pulling the door closed. Beanie stood up and peered over the top of the boxes, her face just regaining colour. "I thought I was caught again," she whispered. "That was too close for comfort."

"I know," Tony agreed, thinking the same thing. He grabbed Beanie's hand. "We'd better get out of here too, before something else happens."

"I think we should follow them," Beanie said, but her voice was hesitant. She was remembering the horror she had felt when she'd been kidnapped last year. She never wanted to go through an experience like that again!

"I don't," Tony said firmly, pulling her toward the office door. "It would be too dangerous." The words died on his lips as he froze in his tracks just inside the doorway. "Sh-h-h," he warned, his finger against his lips. The doorknob on the office door rattled as voices filtered in.

"Oh no," Beanie moaned, her fingers trembling against Tony's arm. "We're in trouble now." Tony and Beanie scrambled behind the stack of boxes in the office as the sound of footsteps stopped just outside the room. Crouching low to the ground between the boxes and the wall, they fought to calm their noisy breathing.

There was limited space and it was difficult to conceal their two growing bodies well. Some body part kept hanging out the sides. It was usually Tony's leg on one side, or Beanie's arm on the other. Tony silently caught Beanie's eye and hugged his arms to his chest, showing her how to make herself smaller. Doing this, she leaned against the wall, her knees drawn up almost to her chin.

Tony tried to copy the same position, but found that his legs were too long. Instead he had to turn sideways, his right shoulder pressing against the wall for support, his left just grazing the stack of boxes. From here he had a good view of the office door, but that meant that he could be seen. Trying to wiggle backward, he bumped into Beanie.

"Stay put," she whispered, looking past Tony. "They're at the door!"

Leaning into the small shadow cast by the light hanging from the ceiling, Tony watched as two men entered the room. He recognized the red-headed man immediately; it was Red Thompson. The other man was wearing a derby, but Tony recognized him as Ted Rogers, one of the other men who had been on stage at the rally.

"That's quite a haul we made today," Red laughed. He was carrying a small cloth bag, which he set on the desk in front of him.

"Look at all this money!" The string rasped against the material and coins jingled. A rustling filled the room as Tony peeked around the boxes. Ted was fanning a fistful of ten-dollar bills in the air. "I'd say you can afford to buy that new hat now, Red!"

Laughing, Red reached across and took several bills. "I think you're right." He laid the money down on the desk.

Tony and Beanie heard the scrape of wood against wood—the sound of a drawer being opened. "It's gone," Ted stated as he frantically searched the desk area, opening every drawer. Dropping to his hands and knees, he searched under the desk, his hat falling unnoticed to the floor. "The money box is gone."

"It can't be," Red said. "Nobody would be stupid enough to steal from us." He laughed as if he had told the funniest joke in the world.

"I tell you, it's gone," Ted confirmed as he jumped to his feet. He thumped the drawer shut and pulled another one open. "It's not here."

Silence stretched across the room as the two men stared at one another. "You gave those two clowns a key," Red accused, shaking a finger under Ted's nose. "Why did you do that? I told you you couldn't trust those two."

"They're too cowardly. They wouldn't have the guts to do something like this."

"Then who did?" Red asked. "I think it's their

boss, that Mean-Eyed Max. He just wants in on our action!"

"Well, we are making a killing here in this small town," Ted argued. "Who'd have thought a place called Moose Jaw would get so excited about the Klan? I can't believe how many people came to the rally! We haven't had those kinds of crowds since we left the southern States last fall."

Tony's legs were cramped, his right foot falling asleep. Pins and needles pricked at his toes and he tried wriggling them to get the circulation going again. He wished the men would just get out of the office and go look for their money! He didn't know how much longer he'd be able to hold this awkward position.

"It's too bad we're not going to hang around much longer to help organize them into a real KKK group. We'll just show them a few more tricks of the trade and move on to greener pastures west of here–as soon as I catch up with that Mean-Eyed Max and have a word with him." He pounded his fist into the palm of his other hand, the sound sharp. "Let's go get him right now!"

The men hurried out of the office, leaving the door ajar. Their voices grew fainter as they walked away. Tony breathed a sigh of relief and wriggled out from behind the boxes. "Whew," he breathed, stretching his calf muscles. "If I had to stay in that awful position for one more minute, I think I'd have collapsed!"

"Talking to yourself, kid?" a voice growled from the doorway. "What are you doing in here?"

Yelping in fear, Tony jumped and whirled around, his heart pounding. It felt as if it would beat its way out of his chest. "N-nothing," he stammered, backing away. His back hit the desk and he stood cowering up at Red Thompson and Ted Rogers.

Red's moustache outlined his scowl and bushy eyebrows made his eyes look fierce and angry. They quivered when he spoke. "It's a good thing we came back. Who are you working for?" he demanded, his voice falling like frozen icicles on Tony's ears.

Ted glowered down at Tony from his great height. "I just come back to get my hat and look what I find–a snoopy kid nosing around where he doesn't belong. How long have you been here anyway?"

"N-not long," Tony whispered, his voice quivering. His fists were clenched behind his back, his fingers digging into his palms. He willed himself not to look in Beanie's direction. He didn't want to give the men any reason to search the room.

"Long enough, I'd say," Red guessed. "This'll teach you to stick your nose into other people's business, kid." In a fluid motion he reached for his hat with one hand and grabbed Tony's arm with the other, twisting it painfully behind his back. "You're coming with us, kid!"

Beanie watched in terror as Tony struggled to free himself. Her first instinct was to scream and shout; find something to throw and get Tony free. Common sense told her that the best thing she could do was to stay quiet until the men left and then go get help quickly.

Scarcely daring to breathe, Beanie stayed crouched behind the boxes. She could hear the scuffling sound of footsteps against the cement as the men half dragged Tony away. Where were they taking him? In her haste to see where they were going, Beanie barged out of the office door and into the darkened warehouse, blindly following the sound.

"Don't take me down there!" she heard Tony shout. There was the sound of a door banging open and then the thump of footsteps descending.

"Where are you taking me?" Tony yelled again and Beanie figured he was trying to get the bad guys to talk so that she would have an idea of where to rescue him from.

"Quiet kid," Red thundered ominously, "or I'll really give you something to yell about. We're just taking a little trip down here into the tunnels. No one would ever think to look for you here. Most people have never *heard* of the tunnels in Moose Jaw, and half of those who *have* heard don't believe the story. Thank goodness!"

"Yeah," Ted added. His voice sounded hollow, as if he were speaking in a deep well. "That really works in our favour. We use the tunnels for all kinds of things. There's even a secret meeting of sorts going on down here to –"

"Shut up!" Red barked. "Don't give so much information. You never know who might be listening..."

Suddenly Beanie heard the footsteps reverse and come pounding back toward her. They grew louder and more insistent with each step. She whirled toward the huge doors that opened onto Ominica Street and flew like the wind, feeling as if the white ghosts from the rally were hot on her heels.

"Hey, you!" Red called into the night. "If you want to see your friend again, don't send the cops. Don't tell anyone about this, or else..."

THE ATTACK

Andrea sat, red-faced and silent, as Vance's mother, Viola, paced back and forth in front of her, ignoring Baby Alan, who played noisily on the floor nearby. He stacked his toy blocks three or four high and then bashed them down with a sweep of his hand, laughing with delight as they scattered about the floor.

"Just whatever were you thinking, young lady?" Viola demanded. Not waiting for an answer, she continued to lecture. "I want to speak to your parents! You are misguided! You don't want to join an organization like that!"

Throwing up her hands, she turned to her husband, tripping over the offending Klan outfit Andrea had dropped as soon as they came in the door. She kicked it with her foot, sending it skidding across the room and through Alan's bedroom door.

"Does she actually want to belong to a group which wears hideous outfits like this? Talk some sense into her, Mr. Paterson, while I try to calm down!" She fanned herself with her hand. "Whatever is this world coming to when decent young women are so muddled?!"

Officer Paterson cleared his throat looking uncomfortable and fatherly at the same time. "You do understand, don't you, my dear, that this is a bad organization? It's not something that a young lady should want to be involved with."

He looked so concerned, his eyes warm and worried at the same time, that Andrea couldn't even meet his gaze. Head bowed, she sat, staring at her fingers clenched tightly in her lap. She was embarrassed they would even think that she would actually want to join a group like that! The urge to tell them that she had gone undercover to help Vance get a story was overwhelming, but she pursed her lips firmly together and kept quiet. Didn't people do this kind of surveillance work in the 1920s?

"We'll go for now," Mr. Paterson said, seeing how upset she was. He took his wife's arm. "I think Andrea needs to do a lot of thinking about this incident." He patted her shoulder, then slipped his hat on. "I've gotten a handyman to come and fix the window," he told Rosie. Sighing heavily, Mrs. Paterson allowed herself to be led down the stairs.

"Wait!" Andrea called, "it's not what you think." But she was too late. The Patersons had already disappeared out the door.

Silence filtered through the kitchen. It was so quiet that Andrea could hear the clock ticking between her shallow breaths. Baby Alan, finally realizing something was wrong, toddled over to Andrea's chair and held up his arms to her. Gathering him close, she kissed his chubby cheek, cuddling him on her lap. He reached up, his baby fingers stroking her cheek. "Sh-h-h," he whispered, his eyes intent on hers. "Sh-h-h. It's oday."

Giggling in spite of herself, Andrea gave Alan a squeeze. She sighed deeply, feeling her lungs expand and contract. "I wish life was as simple for me as it is for you, Baby."

Rosie plunked a cup of steaming tea on the table. "Here, this should help you feel better. Now do you want to tell me what this is really about?"

Wondering how much she should tell, Andrea remained silent, thoughts and feelings battling inside her.

Pulling up a chair, Rosie sank down beside her and took her hand, squeezing it lightly. "I know you, Andrea," she said firmly. "There's no way on earth you would ever decide to join the Ku Klux Klan. Not unless you were forced to – or felt you were helping someone, somehow. Though how becoming a member of that group would ever help anyone, I don't know..." Her voice trailed off uncertainly.

"Oh Rosie," Andrea's voice quivered. "Thank goodness you know me so well! Everything's in such a mess. I don't know what to do!"

Moving her chair closer, Rosie put both arms around Andrea, making soothing sounds. "You can tell me anything, Andrea, you know that. Talk to me."

Andrea wrestled with her conscience for a few more moments, but the need to share her problems with someone she could trust took over. "I've been keeping this inside for so long I feel like I'm going to burst! Maybe you can help me!" Not caring that she was telling about the future, Andrea talked. It was like a dam of emotion bursting over the barricade. The words and feelings just poured out of her.

In her fascination with Andrea's tale, Rosie absent-mindedly claimed the tea and drank it. "Whew," she declared when at last Andrea fell silent. "I guess knowing the future can sometimes be a heavy burden. I can see why you've been so unsettled and upset by it. And now I can understand why you did it."

Shuddering, Andrea mopped at her face with the hanky. Alan wiggled down from her lap and went back to playing with his blocks on the floor. "I'm just so worried about Grandpa. I don't know how he's doing and I'm stuck here in the past. I have to get that notebook soon!"

"Don't worry," Rosie said, patting her arm. "We'll find a way. Just let me think about it for a bit."

Andrea sighed. "I don't know if I'm happy or sad that the Patersons found out." She smiled as she related how Viola had grabbed her by the arm, horror and indignation written all over her face. She had marched her back to Rosie's place, lecturing her the whole way. "It's almost funny."

Glancing at Rosie, she giggled. It was a musical sound that bounced around the somber room, dispelling the gloom. Rosie watched for a moment, a smile dancing on her lips, then she too began to chuckle.

It felt good to laugh and Andrea and Rosie let loose as big bellyfuls of laughter echoed around the kitchen. Alan stood watching uncertainly, his finger in his mouth. Finally, he joined them. Throwing back his head, he began to chortle, his tiny teeth gleaming.

Finally the merriment died down. "I've got to think about getting supper on," Rosie commented. Footsteps sounded on the stairs. "That sounds like Vance," Rosie commented.

"I hope he's had a better day than me." Andrea rushed to open the door. "Remember, Rosie, don't say anything."

"I promise," Rosie agreed.

"I'm going to walk over to get Sarah and escort her home for supper. Does anyone want to come with me?" Vance asked as he entered the room. He seemed in a more cheerful mood, a slight smile on his lips and his blue eyes twinkling.

The expression on his face was one Andrea had seen at least a hundred times on Grandpa's face over the years and it made her heart lurch.

Baby Alan ran over to Vance and stood pulling on his pant leg, vying for his attention. "Up, Ban!" he demanded, yanking on Vance's pant legs. "Up! Up! Alan up!"

"He wants to go too." Rosie smiled fondly at her son. "Would you mind taking him while I finish up with supper?"

"Go too," Alan echoed happily.

Bending, Vance scooped him up into his arms. "I love taking Baby Alan for walks, and Sarah will be so glad to see him." He threw Alan up into the air and caught him as he squealed in delight. "Come on, little man." He settled Alan on his shoulder and turned to leave. "Coming Andrea?"

Andrea felt torn, debating whether or not she should stay to help with supper. More than anything, she wanted to tell Vance about her afternoon's adventures.

"You go ahead," Rosie said softly, noticing Andrea's dilemma. "I can manage things here. We'll eat around 7:30," she added. "If you see Beanie and Tony, bring them along too. I don't want them unsupervised for too long. You never know what kind of trouble they'll get into."

"I'll do the dishes," Andrea promised, quickly joining Vance as he disappeared down the stairs. This might be just the opportunity she needed to find out more about his notebook. Her mood lightened as she stepped through the doorway and out onto the porch, shutting the door with its broken window behind her.

It was a cloudy, muggy evening. The sun's setting rays were trapped behind a thick band of dark clouds, making it seem later than it was. The streets were deserted. A faint breeze fanned their faces, bringing with it the savory smell of dinners cooking. "Where is everybody?" Andrea asked as they walked down Ominica Street. The huge warehouse loomed ahead, silent and foreboding.

"Everyone eats at six o'clock on the nose around here," Vance commented as they neared the warehouse, the empty trucks still parked beside the large swinging doors.

"It sure feels funny to be out when no one else is," Andrea said.

"Eerie," Vance added absently. "I like that word, eerie. I'll have to try to remember to use it in something I'm writing." He was talking more to himself than to Andrea as he ambled along, Alan bouncing contentedly on his shoulders. "That's what it feels like," he said, coming out of his reverie, "kind of mysterious and unnerving."

"It sure does," Andrea agreed, scanning the street as they rounded the corner and turned onto Main Street. She searched the road, looking several blocks south to the train station. Nothing moved. It felt like they were in the middle of a movie set ready for action. The only thing missing was the actors. Goosebumps spread up her forearms. "'The tension was so thick you could cut it with a knife,'" she quoted. "I'm sure I read that somewhere. That's what it feels like: tense and –"

" –and apprehensive," Vance said, smiling. "I like that word too. Don't you, Alan?" He jiggled the child up and down on his shoulders.

"Me too," Alan echoed. He giggled with glee, his tiny fists clenched around Vance's hair, and the other two joined in.

"He's sure smart," Andrea commented, reaching up to pat his back. "He's talking a lot."

They walked past the large windows in the Klan office, the posters leering out at them. Andrea suppressed a nervous giggle as she told Vance about the funny and embarrassing incident with his parents that afternoon. "You should have seen your mother grab me and drag me to Rosie's. She really thinks I'm terrible now."

"My mother did that?" He laughed in surprise. "She must feel as strongly as I do about that organization. Don't worry," he told Andrea, leaning over to jostle her with his shoulder. "I'll explain everything to my parents. They'll understand."

"Don' worry," Alan parroted happily, leaning toward Andrea, his lips puckered for a kiss. Andrea couldn't help but smile.

She let the matter drop, glad that Vance wasn't mad at her. "So, can I still have a look at your poetry and stories? I did exactly what you asked, and I'll tell you everything I've learned about the Klan."

Baby Alan was vying for Vance's attention and he didn't have a chance to respond to Andrea's question. Or maybe he didn't want to answer it, Andrea thought, wondering how she would ever get her hands on the notebook.

They neared Fairford Street, the clock on the town hall shining out across the gloomy sky. "I love walking in olden-days Moose Jaw," Andrea said, her eyes feasting on the old brick buildings marching up and down Main Street. If she turned around, she knew that she would see the Hazelton Hotel not too far back, with the big old church standing near it. Those buildings and many others were still standing in present day Moose Jaw.

Not one car had driven up or down Main Street in the time they'd been walking. The streets and sidewalks were still devoid of people. "It's like a bad storm is coming," she commented, looking around. She shivered then as a finger of fear travelled up her spine, leaving the hairs on the back of her neck standing at attention. "Where are Tony and Beanie? I haven't seen them since this morning, have you?"

Vance shook his head. "Now that you mention it, I haven't either. I don't like it when those two disappear. You never know what they could be getting into."

A ghost of a premonition flashed through her mind. "I think they're in some kind of trouble," she whispered, clutching Vance's arm.

"We'll go look for them as soon as we get Sarah home safely," he promised, looking grim. "You could be wrong, you know."

"Maybe," Andrea agreed softly and she tried, unsuccessfully, not to worry.

The train station loomed ahead. Even though it was still a few blocks away, it looked immense and inviting. Its lights shone into the gloomy evening air, welcoming visitors and tourists with its cozy atmosphere. The large oval face of the clock was lit, its big black arms pointing at the eleven and the seven. Almost seven o'clock.

Suddenly a series of booms filled the air like dropping bombs. The sounds echoed, reverberating between the buildings, as the ground trembled beneath their feet. A car squealed its tires, its engine gunning as it careened around the corner and shot up the street toward them. "Get down!" Vance yelled, crouching low to the ground behind a parked car, Baby Alan clutched tightly to his chest.

"What was that?!" Andrea shouted, scooting in beside Vance as the car hurtled toward them. The yellow beams from its headlights bounced up and down, shining bright spotlights into the ground and then up into the cloudy sky.

Vance peered over the hood of the parked car as the racing vehicle rocketed up the street. "That's the same car," he said as he squinted after it. "And I think I saw the red-headed guy driving it."

"It was the Klan," Andrea confirmed.

Vance tensed suddenly, as realization sluiced through his mind. "Oh no," he whispered, his face sickly white. Panic-stricken, he thrust Alan into Andrea's trembling arms and stumbled to his feet and raced toward Wong's Café.

"Sarah!"

BIG TROUBLE

Andrea lurched to her feet. Grasping the now screaming child closely, she raced for River Street. What had happened? Was it a bomb? Reaching the intersection, she braced herself and looked toward Wong's Café.

Where once there'd been large plate glass windows, huge shards of glass gleamed menacingly in the evening air. Glass was strewn all over the ground. Some of the windows were completely void of glass. Others had huge and jagged holes where big rocks, or something, had been hurled through them. Bits and pieces of glass, covered the sidewalks, though most of it must have fallen inside.

Andrea watched as Vance flung open the door to the café, frantically searching for Sarah. He called her name over and over again, his voice high-pitched and frantic with worry.

Picking her way carefully through the glass, Andrea crossed the street. She was glad to be wearing her thick-soled running shoes and not the thin-soled olden-days shoes. Her feet were much better protected. Baby Alan had calmed down a little and now whimpered quietly, his face buried in the large collar of her dress. She clutched him to her chest, not sure who she was trying to comfort, Alan or herself.

Through the empty window, Andrea watched as Mr. Wong rose unsteadily to his feet, an ugly red gash on his forehead. Mrs. Wong had come in from the back and was talking hysterically in Chinese, tears running down her face. She hugged Mr. Wong and then scrambled behind the restaurant counter. She returned within seconds with a clean white tea towel. Pressing it to his head, she checked carefully for glass in the booth furthest from the windows and then gently pushed him down into the seat.

"Sarah!" Vance found her cowering under one of the tables. Grabbing her up into his arms, he hugged her fiercely to him and then pulled back. "Are you all right?" He inspected her carefully for cuts and bruises. "Oh no, you're hurt! Quick," he called to Mrs. Wong, "bring me a towel!" A long jagged cut ran down Sarah's left arm; her sleeve, torn away, dangled from her elbow.

Andrea saw rivers of tears rush down Sarah's cheeks. She was oblivious to her wound. "I was so scared," she sobbed, her voice carrying out into the night. "There were loud booms and then glass seemed to be raining down on us! Thank goodness all of the pupils had gone home already. Mr. Wong was just walking me to the door." She buried her head in Vance's shoulder, trembling uncontrollably.

Andrea moved closer to the building, crunching the glass under their feet. "Stay outside," Vance warned.

Suddenly Beanie appeared out of nowhere, running wildly across the street. "Andrea!" she yelled, her face white with fear. "Andrea!" She stopped dead in her tracks when her senses registered the mess of glass on the street in front of her. "What happened?"

"Never mind now, Beanie," Vance ordered from Sarah's side. "Just run and get Ol' Doc Anderson. Tell him to hurry. Sarah is hurt and Mr. Wong is cut badly. Then go get Pa. He said he had a meeting at the police station tonight."

"But Vance," Beanie protested weakly, her features so pasty white that Andrea was sure she'd faint. "Something terrible has happened."

"I know that." Vance was losing his patience, the words spitting out of his mouth like sharp nails. "Go get Ol' Doc and Pa."

"But Vance–" she tried once again, her knees buckling as she sat down heavily on the sidewalk.

Andrea went to her, awkwardly bending down with Baby Alan still in her arms. "Are you all right?" She smoothed Beanie's hair out of her face with one hand, while keeping a firm grip on Alan's chubby arm.

Beanie's mouth moved as she gulped back loud sobs. She looked up at Andrea. Large tears slid down her cheeks as a silent message passed between the two.

"Tony." The bottom dropped out of Andrea's stomach as the world began to spin.

"He's kidnapped," Beanie sobbed. "The Klansmen grabbed him."

"Oh no!" Andrea felt the blood rush from her head, afraid that *she* was going to faint. Why did this have to happen now? Didn't she already have enough to worry about?

"What's going on out there?" Vance called. His voice had a steel edge to it. "I thought I told Beanie to get moving!"

"It's Tony," Andrea managed, trying to get her emotions under control. "He's been kidnapped."

"Kidnapped?!" Vance shouted, his eyes boring into Beanie. Even at that distance she could feel the heat of his anger. "I suppose you two were in the tunnels?" His voice was brittle with accusation.

"The warehouse," Beanie admitted, staring at her feet. She looked as if she wished the ground would open up and swallow her, taking her away from this terrible moment.

"I thought I warned you –" Vance began, then checked himself. "We have to deal with this crisis first," he informed Beanie and Andrea. "We'll get to Tony as soon as possible, I promise."

The girls nodded, letting Vance take charge. "Beanie, go and get Ol' Doc and Pa." Beanie didn't wait to be told twice. "Andrea, take Alan home. Tell Rosie what happened. Have her bring the camera too. Finally there might be something we can pin on that awful Klan group!"

"Why do you say that, Vance?" Andrea asked.

"Nobody else would do this kind of thing. Besides," he held up a huge rock. A note was tied to it. "It looks like they left their signature."

"What about Sarah?" Andrea asked. "Will she be okay?" She wished she could get into the café to see for herself.

"Doc Anderson will have to sew up her arm and have a good look at the rest of her, just in case," Vance replied. "Go get Rosie, and hurry," he ordered tersely and Andrea obeyed, resolutely keeping her thoughts away from Tony and the kind of trouble he might be in.

The trip back to Rosie's seemed like a nightmare. Main Street was still deserted, although Andrea noticed some people coming out of the hotels along River Street. They clung together, gaping at the sight and talking loudly.

Night had fallen. Shadows stretched across the sidewalk, dark and foreboding. Doorways were black pools of terror, fertile places for her wild imagination. She envisioned long black tentacles snaking out to entrap her and Baby Alan. Ghostly white figures danced in her head, leering at her through empty eye sockets. Terror grabbed hold of her and shook her.

She tried to run, but the baby jiggled up and down, giving her an awkward gait that slowed her down even more than walking. Be sensible, she ordered herself. Get your imagination under control. But the ghostly figures nipped at her heels as they chased her up Main Street, pulling on the hem of her dress until she wasn't sure what was real anymore.

Ominica Street came into sight and Andrea rounded the corner, keeping her eyes away from the windows of the KKK office. If something was going on there, she didn't want to know about it. A movement near the large side doors of the warehouse caught her attention and she flattened herself and Alan against the side of the building, hoping the dark shadows would make them invisible, glad that Alan was quiet now.

Andrea watched as one large door was opened. A car was wheeled swiftly inside and the door pulled shut. Three men stood outside the door, but it was too dark for her to see their faces. "I don't think they'll come looking for us here," a voice said, "but just in case, tell them to put the car in the far back corner and cover it with a tarp." That voice belonged to Mr. Robertson! She would have recognized it anywhere.

"I'd say we're in the clear," another voice added, laughter edging the words. "I hope we taught that woman and Wong a lesson. Next time we'll aim and be more accurate." Red Thompson, Andrea decided. Even though she couldn't see his hair, she could see that he was the only one without a hat.

"Yeah," Mr. Robertson said. "It's lucky we just wanted to scare them."

"Don't be too cheerful," Ted warned as he opened the door. "We still have that kid to deal with." Muttering angrily, the men disappeared inside, leaving Andrea huddling against the building in fright. She knew just who they were talking about!

How long should she wait? How long would it be until the men came back outside? Would they have Tony with them? Not sure what to do, Andrea decided to hurry on to Rosie's. She quickly crossed the street, trying not to make scuffling noises with her feet. Her scalp tingled with fear and she could feel the tiny hairs quiver. Once safely across the street, she walked as near to the buildings and houses as she could get, hoping to stay in the shadows and undetected.

Half running, half walking, Andrea hurried up the street. This last stretch was the longest; it felt as if she would never arrive. She kept moving forward but nothing seemed to be happening. Would she ever get to Rosie's place?

Finally Andrea saw the cheery lights of Rosie's house blazing into the night. Like a welcoming beacon, the lights greeted her. Reaching out warm friendly rays, the light pulled her into the safety of the house.

Climbing the steps, Andrea felt as if she'd been gone for a hundred years. "Rosie!" she yelled, pushing open the door with its still-broken window. She raced up the stairs, Alan bouncing on her hip. She thought of Sarah and Mr. Wong and Tony, all in dire straits.

"Rosie! Come quickly! There's been big trouble!"

"Let Mean-Eyed Max
Take Care of Him."

Dragging Tony roughly by the arms, Red Thompson and Ted Rogers hurried across the warehouse floor. "What are we going to do with him?" Ted asked.

"Teach him not to nose around in other people's business. Don't you know that curiosity killed the cat, kiddo?" He jerked hard on Tony's arm causing him to stumble, his knees dragging on the coarse floor.

Where are they taking me? Tony wondered. They appeared to be heading toward the back of the warehouse. Suddenly they stopped in front of a shelf. Letting go of Tony with one hand, Ted pushed it aside, revealing a new set of steps. "It's a good thing we had these built when we did. They've sure come in handy lately."

They bumped Tony down the stairs, not caring that he bashed his knees time and again. It seemed that the more he whimpered the worse they treated him. At the end of the staircase, Red Thompson pulled open another door and suddenly they were inside the underground storage area. A few lanterns were lit and Tony could just make out the tunnel entrance leading to Rosie's. There were stacks of boxes and crates placed haphazardly throughout the area.

"It's too bad we can't deal with him now. But there's too much to be done, what with the meeting tonight. Let's just throw him in the storeroom and deal with him later." Skirting the piles of crates, they meandered to the south wall near the Forbidden tunnel.

If only he could get free, Tony thought. Going limp for a few seconds, he let the men take all his weight. "Hey! Cut it out, kid," Red Thompson scowled.

Thinking he could surprise them and perhaps break free, Tony gathered all his strength. He planted his feet firmly on the ground and gave a sudden lurch. Twisting furiously, he almost pulled himself free.

Ted jerked Tony hard again, tightening his grip. "I said, cut it out, kid. Do I need to whack you or what?" He cuffed Tony's ear.

"No cuts or bruises, mind," Red Thompson ordered. "We haven't decided what to do with him yet. Maybe we'll just scare him a little by keeping him for a few days..." He laughed a sinister laugh which chilled Tony to the bone. "Or maybe we'll sic Mean-Eyed Max on him. I heard he got rid of another poor kid who couldn't keep his nose out of trouble. He ended up dead behind the Hazelton. Is that what you want, kid?"

Tony shook his head wildly. They were only threatening him, weren't they? He wasn't so sure. His voice, a petrified lump in his throat, emitted only high, squeaky sounds. Please, he prayed silently. Please, somebody save me!

A door, well camouflaged in the dirt wall, was pushed open and Tony was thrown inside. It was a tiny, dank, windowless room. "Here, tie him up," Red ordered, pulling two lengths of coarse rope out of a box. "Gag him, too." He threw a dirty handkerchief at Tony's feet.

"No gag, please," Tony begged. "I won't call out, I promise."

The bad guys laughed. "Sure, kid. As if we could trust you!"

Ted made short work of the ropes and Tony found himself hog-tied and gagged. He lay on the cold dirt floor watching in terror as the two men left the room, closing the door behind them.

It was so dark Tony could see pinpricks of light in front of his eyes. He heard the men talking in low voices. Someone said, "...Mean-Eyed Max." Chills ran down his spine and he held his breath. He was listening so hard his ears were buzzing.

There was more talk, muffled and indistinct, and then Ted said, "Let's let Mean-Eyed Max take care of him." They shuffled away, their footsteps crunching on the ground.

Terrified for his life, Tony wriggled and squirmed until he was exhausted. Hot and sweaty, he lay still, his breath coming in pants of panic. Andrea will find you, he kept repeating to himself. Vance and Beanie won't let anything happen to you, he chanted.

But what if they couldn't get here in time? What if they didn't know where to look?

With his hands tied behind his back, he didn't have a hope of reaching his fanny pack to get his insulin. He had never been in so much danger in his life. He just prayed someone would find him before it was too late.

WHAT'S HAPPENED TO SARAH?

Rosie met her at the kitchen door, reaching for Baby Alan, a look of alarm on her face. "What is it?"

"It's Sarah," Andrea sputtered, trying to catch her breath. Her sides ached and she doubled over in pain. "And Mr. Wong – the café – it's a wreck. Something terrible has happened." Painfully, Andrea sank to the floor, her legs rubbery, her calf muscles aching. "You need to get to Wong's Café now. Sarah and Mr. Wong are hurt."

With a gasp Rosie jumped into action, a frantic expression on her face. Dashing around the room, she hurried to get ready, pushing her pillbox hat on her head, almost squashing it. It sat askew on her head and under it her hair stuck out in disarray. She madly pulled on her white gloves, her notebook tucked under one arm. She picked Alan up and headed for the door. "Get the camera and tripod, Andrea," she ordered as she brushed past her and hurried down the stairs. "Put them in the car."

Still trying to catch her breath, Andrea grabbed the camera and long-legged tripod and bumped down the stairs after Rosie, trying to be careful. She knew how expensive this old-fashioned equipment was.

"Thanks, Andrea," Rosie said as she kissed Alan and hastily handed him over to Andrea.

Rosie scooted behind the steering wheel, shut the car door with a bang, and adjusted her pillow. She took a closer look at Andrea. "Are you all right?"

"I'm just tired, I guess," Andrea lied, wishing she could tell Rosie the truth; that Tony had been kidnapped and she was scared out of her wits. But the KKK had said to keep it quiet or else, and so she bit her tongue to keep the words locked inside and waved goodbye.

"Try to get some rest," Rosie suggested as she started the car.

Nodding tearfully, Andrea trudged back up the stairs and sat Alan down amidst his pile of blocks. Feeling totally spent, physically and emotionally, she fell into a chair and leaned her head on the kitchen table. Pictures of the devastation at the café danced through her mind and she felt sick with worry and mad with anger. What kind of people would do something like that? What if Mr. Wong and Sarah were really hurt? Where was Tony? Tears leaked out of her eyes and rolled down her cheeks in a flood of despair.

Wanting to offer comfort, Alan marched across the room, his chubby fingers clutching some of his blocks. Reaching into Andrea's lap, he plopped his blocks. "There," he said, smiling up at her.

"Thanks," Andrea smiled weakly, ruffling the baby's hair. Jabbering in baby talk, Alan ran back and scooped up some more blocks. He brought them back and excitedly tossed them into her lap.

Andrea slipped to the floor and mindlessly stacked the blocks for Alan, her mind darting to Wong's Café and then flying back again to the tunnels, wondering where Tony was. What was going on? Why didn't anyone come to tell her what was happening? When would they be able to go look for Tony? Her heart felt sick with worry and as heavy as a lead balloon. This was way too much anxiety for one person to handle.

How long she sat on the floor playing with Alan, Andrea didn't know. Finally the toddler tired out and crawled into her lap, yawning widely. "Let's get you to bed, little man," she whispered, picking him up as he snuggled his head into her shoulder. He didn't protest as she undressed him, changed him, and put him into bed in a cotton undershirt and diaper. Pulling a little blanket up around him, she softly kissed his head. "Good night," she whispered and tiptoed out of the room.

The outside door opened and closed below and Andrea heard voices. "Beanie?" she called. "Beanie, is that you?"

"It's us," Beanie replied breathlessly as the sound of footsteps came slowly up the stairs. "Vance just dropped us off. He's gone back to get more information and to help Rosie take pictures. He said he'd come here as soon as possible and we'd go look for Tony. I'm going to clean Sarah up. Come and help me."

"Are you okay, Sarah?" Andrea asked.

There was a brief mumbled reply, then Beanie said, "She'll be okay. Doc Anderson gave her something for the pain and I think it's made her groggy."

Andrea gathered up the sleeping Baby Alan and went downstairs to join them.

Sarah and Beanie stood in the middle of Sarah's tiny kitchen, uncertain what to do. Andrea came into the lighted room, took one look at Sarah, and gasped. Her head whirled and she felt as if she might be sick. She took the still-sleeping baby into Sarah's room and gently placed him on the bed.

Sarah was a mess. Her hair was dishevelled, sticking out in every direction. Bits of glass, large and small, glinted in the light and Andrea wondered how they would ever get her cleaned up. Fine grains of glass, like sand, were embedded into her clothes and sugar-coated her face and arms. They shone in the light, making Sarah look like a twinkling but deadly fairy princess. Her left arm had been wrapped in several metres of white gauze from her upper arm to the tips of her fingers. It was bent at the elbow.

"I-I don't know where to start," Beanie faltered, her voice weepy as tears glistened in her eyes. The shock was wearing off and suddenly she was a bundle of nerves.

Blinking back tears, Andrea took charge. "Let's put an old sheet down on the floor to try to catch all the glass." Rummaging through the linen closet, she found a sheet and quickly spread it out. She took Sarah's hand and led her onto the cloth. "Let's get this dress off you, first." She spoke as gently as if she was speaking to a child.

Carefully brushing bits of glass away, Andrea undid the buttons. It was the kind of dress that needed to be pulled over the head. She stood back wondering what to do.

"I don't think we should pull this off you, Sarah. I'm worried about glass getting into your eyes." Sarah stood silently and as still as a statue. She was in shock, Andrea realized. Her face was ashen, her eyes pools of fear and horror. Andrea could see that she wouldn't be any help at all.

"I think we'll have to cut it off her." Andrea sighed, her eyes tearing up again. "Get the scissors, Beanie. I don't think there's any other way, and I don't want to risk the chance of getting that glass anywhere near her face."

"You're right," Beanie agreed. She found two pairs of scissors and brought them back. "This reminds me of last year when I had to cut your hair." They giggled and even Sarah smiled, a ghost of a smile that just reached her lips. It felt good to laugh, even under such terrible circumstances.

"We'll have to cut it right up the centre to the neck," Andrea surmised, kneeling down in front of Sarah. "You cut up the back, Beanie and then we'll peel the dress off her. Be careful of the glass. Keep your mouth closed and squint your eyes in case a piece flies up, okay? We don't want any more injuries."

Working carefully, they cut the dress in half. It was a slow process, impeded by the fact that bits of glass kept falling off the dress, or flying at them. Once or twice Sarah swayed and Andrea had to jump to her feet to help steady her.

"We're almost done," she whispered as her scissors neared the neckline. She snipped a few more centimetres and the dress came apart. "There." They laid the scissors down and then carefully peeled the dress away, leaving Sarah standing in her white petticoat.

Dropping both halves of the dress onto the sheet, Andrea sighed in relief. One job was done. She placed a chair in the centre of the sheet. "Sit here, Sarah," she said as Beanie gently guided her to sit. "Your hair is next."

Beanie fetched the comb and brush, and an old towel which she wrapped around Sarah's shoulders. Andrea carefully pulled the hairpins out of Sarah's hair and let it settle around her shoulders. "Most of the glass is near the front of your head and on top. I guess that's because you ducked. It's a good thing you covered your eyes." She shivered picturing Sarah's face cut to ribbons, her eyes sightless. It was a horrible thought!

Working carefully and with painstaking patience, Andrea combed and inspected every centimetre of Sarah's head. When she found a piece of glass, she would gingerly pull it out of the tangle of hair, trying not to cut herself or Sarah. These bits she placed in a small container Beanie had found.

Andrea picked so many bits and pieces of glass from Sarah's hair that she lost count. The work was tedious and her arms felt leaden. She never wanted to be a hairdresser, that was for sure! Her arms wouldn't be able to take it.

It was after midnight by the time Andrea felt certain Sarah's head was free of glass. Sarah had fallen asleep long ago, her head leaning to one side, her mouth open slightly. "I think I got most of it," Andrea murmured, running the brush slowly through

Sarah's hair one more time. "I think we'd better wash your hair, though, just in case."

There was a light tap on the door and Rosie entered while Vance hovered just outside on the threshold. Further behind him Andrea could see Officer Paterson. "Is Sarah all right?" Rosie asked, stepping into the room.

"She's sleepy and indecent just now," Beanie retorted, springing forward to block Vance's view. "She's only wearing her petticoat," she whispered to Rosie as she entered the room.

"Where's Alan?" Rosie asked.

"In Sarah's bedroom, asleep," Andrea said. "Is that Officer Paterson out there?" He stepped closer. "I'm glad you're here," she told him.

"After what's happened tonight, I've stationed a police officer in front of the house. We're not taking any chances. I'm just sorry I didn't think of it sooner. Maybe none of this would have happened if we'd taken those threatening messages more seriously."

"Well, thank goodness no one was hurt badly. Sarah will be fine and Mr. Wong is recovering nicely," Rosie added.

"Can I spend the night?" Beanie boldly asked.

"Not tonight," Officer Paterson started to say, but Andrea interrupted him.

"Please let her stay," Andrea begged. "I-I don't get to see her too often."

Rosie nodded absently, her mind still on Sarah. "That's fine with me, and I'm sure Viola will be fine with it."

Officer Paterson shrugged his shoulder in defeat. "If it's all right with Rosie, it's all right with me. I'll let your ma know. Just stay out of trouble."

Sighing, Beanie nodded, feeling tears begin to threaten. Too bad she and Tony hadn't thought of that earlier.

"I'm going to the station to file a report," Officer Paterson commented. "I'm sure Sarah is going to be fine." He settled his hat on his head. "Mind Rosie now, Beanie, I'm counting on you." He squeezed her shoulder and headed down the stairs. "Oh, by the way, can one of you bring me that hat tomorrow? It might just come in handy in the investigation."

"Sure, Pa," Beanie readily agreed, wondering where the hat was. "T-Tony had it last," she stuttered, her voice clogged with emotion. What she wanted to do more than anything right now, was to throw herself into her father's arms and cry, begging him to save Tony, but she knew she couldn't do it. Red Thompson had sounded so mean that she was sure he would murder Tony if he thought he'd been tricked. Instead, she clenched her fingers into tight fists of control, willing herself not to cry.

"Good night," Officer Paterson called and the outside door shut with a dull thud.

"We'll just let Sarah get some sleep," Rosie said softly, seeing that Vance was still upset. He hovered at the doorway, his soft-brimmed hat squashed between anxious fingers. "Rest is the best medicine of all."

Vance pulled something out of his jacket. "Give her this, just so she knows I'm thinking of her." He handed Rosie a black leather-bound notebook. "Tell her to read the new pieces I've been working on, if she's up to it. It might help take her mind off things for a while."

Andrea gasped aloud, then quickly clamped her mouth shut when Vance looked at her, a puzzled expression on his face. She watched, frozen as a statue, as Rosie took the book. It was Vance's notebook; the one with all of his short stories and poems! She wanted to yank it out of Rosie's hands and run like the wind back to the present. Instead, she stood woodenly as Rosie absently held the book, her mind obviously still on Sarah.

Andrea watched as Rosie casually set the notebook down on the kitchen counter and then turned toward her. She looked questioningly at Andrea. "Are you all right?" She asked, her voice full of concern. "You look like you've seen a ghost!"

I have seen a ghost, Andrea thought to herself, working hard to keep her eyes off the notebook. She didn't want to cause suspicion, and a plan was already at work in her mind. She would grab the notebook as soon as Rosie and Sarah were occupied.

"I-I'm okay," Andrea stuttered, trying to focus her mind on Sarah. "I was going to help Sarah wash her hair," Andrea said.

Sarah roused herself enough to speak. "I think that medicine knocked me out. But I think I can manage by myself now," she said weakly.

"I'm going to help you," Rosie declared, her arms akimbo. "You could have been hit on the head and not even know it, and you're sure not acting like yourself at all. My goodness, it's late! Sarah and I will be just fine." Rosie tenderly helped Sarah out of the room. "Vance," she called. "I'll be up later to write a story for the paper tomorrow. And you'll write one too?"

"Of course," Vance agreed, coming out of his reverie with a start and getting down to business. "But I have something to do first. I can tell that it's going to be a late night." He shut the door, taking Andrea with him and leaving Rosie to tend to Sarah.

"We've left Tony for too long already," he said quietly. "Where do you think he is, Beanie? Where did you last see him?"

Quickly, Beanie explained about the scene in the warehouse office and how Red and Ted had grabbed Tony. "It sounded as if they went into the tunnels," she added, tears filling her eyes. "I wanted to follow, but I was too afraid to, after what happened to me last year."

Andrea agreed. "You did the right thing," she admitted, even though it was her little brother who was missing. "I just hope we can find him before they do something awful to him."

"Do we have a plan?" Beanie asked, her blue eyes mirrors of fear and doubt.

Slowly, Vance and Andrea shook their heads. "Come on, let's think," Vance ordered, heading up the stairs to Rosie's. "We need to come up with a plan. We can't just go barging out into the night and hope things will work in our favour."

Sighing, Andrea and Beanie trudged slowly up the stairs following Vance. Andrea was mentally exhausted and emotionally drained. She felt as if she hadn't slept in a whole week and she wondered if she would ever sleep again! Everything seemed to be moving in slow motion; as if she was under water. She was getting more and more worried about Tony. They had to think of a plan, and soon.

Vance opened the door to Rosie's place. Silence greeted them as they stepped into the room, the toy blocks still strewn across the floor, dirty dishes scattered on the table and counter.

Though she was weary, Andrea picked up the baby's toys and put them in the box. Then she set about washing the dishes and tidying up the kitchen.

"What are you doing?" Vance asked, his voice irritated. "We need to think! The dishes can wait!"

"It helps me think," Andrea retorted as she wiped the table viciously with the dishcloth, her emotions in overdrive. The truth was, her mind was blocked, locked on a horror-filled picture of Tony tied up and gagged in the darkest part of the tunnels. How would they ever find him? What if it took days? Would he be able to reach his insulin in his fanny pack? Was his fanny pack still with him? What if he died?

The endless questions filled Andrea with despair. She felt tears so close that they flooded into her throat, almost choking her. With Herculean effort, she pushed her fears away. She knew they would save Tony, somehow; it was just a matter of time!

There was a commotion at the door and then knocking. "It's the KKK!" Beanie whispered, her eyes filled with terror. "They're coming for us."

"Sh-h-h," Vance ordered, looking uneasy. The knocking was more insistent this time.

Andrea agreed with Beanie and pulled her into the shadow of Rosie's bedroom while Vance carefully opened the door. Mr. Wong stood on the steps, his hat in his hands. He had a huge white bandage wrapped around his head. His face looked pale despite his dark skin, but his eyes were fierce and determined.

"Mr. Wong!" Andrea exclaimed, staring at the bandage. "Shouldn't you be in bed?"

Bowing slightly, Mr. Wong smiled sadly. "I am

fine. I came as soon as I could. I am here because my friend Tony needs help. I overheard Miss Beanie telling you this terrible news; that is how I found out. We must find him. He is in danger!"

"Yes," Andrea agreed, tears suddenly spurting into her eyes. She had been brave all night, but now exhaustion and worry overwhelmed her and she sobbed brokenly. "We don't have a plan."

MR. WONG TO THE RESCUE!

Mr. Wong quickly laid out his plan. "I know there is a meeting in the underground area beneath the warehouse tonight. I heard several of those Klansmen talking when I was walking down Main Street. I stay in the shadows and listen like a tiny bird or mouse – invisible. They are loud and brazen, like monkeys craving attention. They sometimes do not realize how loud they are and how much a quiet bird or mouse like me will hear." He smiled proudly.

"They are dressing in costume to have this meeting. They are deciding which families and businesses to attack next and then they will carry out their dastardly deeds in disguise so that no one will recognize them.

"We need to get into that meeting unseen. I'm sure someone will say something about Tony. If not, the inside person can search the building and get into the underground area as a Klansman and lead those awful people into the Windy tunnel where the rest of us will be waiting. I only wish..." Mr. Wong hesitated, then shook his head, speaking to himself. "I think that is impossible."

"What is?" Andrea asked.

"I was just wishing for one of those dreadful costumes. I cannot show up at their meeting, being Chinese, or I may become a target again. And I think that Vance would have no luck, either, as he is easily identified as newspaper reporter. Miss Beanie is too young yet."

"That leaves –" Mr. Wong looked pointedly at Andrea. "You are a brave sister. Tony has boasted of your travels and adventures in these tunnels. You must be brave once again for Tony. Can you do that?"

Pulling herself together, Andrea nodded. "Yes, I can, and Mr. Wong," she hurried across the room, "we do have a costume." She pulled it from the corner where Viola had kicked it. "I pretended to join the Klan to get information so that Vance can write some newspaper articles, which will expose the group."

Gingerly touching it with only two fingers, Andrea dangled the costume in front of her. "Who gets to wear it?"

Silence fell upon the room as Andrea looked from face to face. They all stared at her, the answer blazing in their eyes. "It's a girl's costume," Vance reminded her. "And it fits you."

"Yes," Andrea said dryly.

"It looks like you're going to your first KKK meeting," Beanie announced.

"Do I have to wear this thing?" Andrea sighed. "I don't even want to touch it! I hate what it stands for!"

"It's the only way we can think of to get close to Tony without putting anyone into too much danger...unless you have another idea?" Vance asked innocently.

Darn it, Andrea thought. He knew she didn't have another plan and that time was of the essence. Swallowing her trepidation, she nodded. "All right." She would do anything to save her little brother, even wear that hateful costume. "So, what's the plan?"

"You must go in disguise to the meeting tonight," Mr. Wong said, his voice apologetic. "They are meeting first in their offices on the corner, but then they are going down into the storage area. You must get into the storage area and look for Tony and then lure the Klansmen into the Windy tunnel. We will enter from the Hazelton Hotel and be waiting. They will not harm any family tonight, if I can help it." He looked grim, determination shining in his eyes.

"I overheard them talking about attacking those who live in Garlic Heights. They plan to burn a cross in someone's yard. We must stop this before it starts."

"But how am I supposed to lure them into the Windy tunnel?" Andrea asked, bewildered. It seemed like an impossible task.

Silence stretched around the room as they racked their brains, trying to come up with an idea. "Oh, you'll think of something," Beanie finally cried, flapping her hands like Aunt Bea in distress.

"Throw something to distract them," Vance advised, "then run. You've done that before."

"That's not much help," Andrea muttered under her breath. "Oh well, I'll do my best." She fingered the heavy cotton material, then pulled the outfit over her head. It caught on the sweatshirt she was wearing, binding and bunching at her elbows. It felt bulky and heavy, the hem falling to her ankles.

"You'd better roll up your jeans," Vance advised. "Someone might spot them as you're walking and become suspicious."

Bending, Andrea rolled up her jeans until the worn material bulged just under her knees. She could cope with the hideous dress, but the hood was something else again. Willing herself not to be sick, she pulled it over her head. The material bunched at her shoulders, blocking out all light except for that coming in through the eyeholes, which she adjusted until she could see out.

"I feel awful in this," she whispered, "This costume feels sinister and evil, like it's full of hate."

Taking a deep breath, she forced those thoughts away.

"Wish me luck," she said, heading for the door, tripping over the long costume as she moved. "I'll be bringing the Klansmen down the Windy tunnel, I hope. You just make sure to be there."

'Vance and I are leaving right now," Mr. Wong responded. He looked pointedly at Beanie.

"I'll stay and look after Baby Alan," Beanie said meekly.

Mr. Wong nodded. "Good luck," he said to Andrea. His hand reached out as if to pat her shoulder and then withdrew without touching her. Andrea understood that. She wouldn't touch this hateful uniform with a ten-foot pole either if she could help it.

"Hey, you might need this," Beanie said, picking up something from the floor. It was the membership card Andrea had filled out. "Who's Doreen Smith?"

"Me," Andrea said, taking the card and sticking it in her pocket. "I just couldn't give them my real name." Feeling less than human in the ghastly outfit, Andrea hurried down the stairs and out into the night. She wanted to get this job over and done with as soon as possible. Then she'd burn the outfit, she decided. She never wanted to see it again, ever.

ANDREA INCOGNITO

Andrea rushed out of the house and down Ominica Street toward the KKK office. Wearing the costume made her feel dirty; like the vilest criminal. She didn't know whether to run fast and get there in order to get the job done quickly, so she could take off the offending outfit, or to creep silently along so no one would see her. Not that anyone would recognize her, she thought, looking down at the heavy costume. It was stifling hot inside and constraining too. She wondered how she would ever run when the time came.

The plan sounded simple enough, she thought, as she half stumbled down the street toward the warehouse building. But a million things could go wrong. What if she got found out? What if she couldn't get anyone to follow her? And, most importantly, what if she couldn't find Tony?

These thoughts and more chased her like demons all the way to Main Street. She could see a number of other ghostly white figures moving silently through the dark. Because of the length of the outfits, they appeared to glide over the ground rather than walk, and this added to the ghoulish appearance.

Lights blazed from the windows of the KKK office, beckoning people inside. Reminding herself that she was only wearing the costume as a means of finding Tony, Andrea turned the corner and walked toward the door. She wasn't a real member of this group and she never would be. Glancing into the windows she saw the room was crowded with about twenty people wearing the costumes. It looked like a ghostly tea party, she thought, and she chuckled to herself.

Pushing the door open, she stepped into the room and looked for some place unobtrusive to stand. "Just a minute," a voice called behind her. Andrea turned around to find a tall, white-draped figure standing nearby. "I need to see your membership card."

Thanking her lucky stars that Beanie had encouraged her to take it, Andrea wiggled around in the costume trying to pull the card out of her pocket. "Here it is," she said handing it over.

The anonymous person took it and held it up to his eyes so that he could read it. "Doreen Smith," he read. "Welcome," he said, giving her back the card. "We just want to be careful of who attends this meeting tonight."

Andrea wasn't interested in the least in the meeting. She only wanted to find a way to get into the tunnels. She was certain that was where Tony was. She would just bide her time and stay with the group until she saw or heard something suspicious, then she would go investigate. That was her plan. It sounded kind of lame, even to her own hopeful heart, but it was the best she could do.

Everyone seemed to be milling about, chatting with one another as they waited for the meeting to begin. How did they tell who was who? Standing against the wall, she merely observed the commotion at first. After a few minutes of confusion, she began to distinguish one KKK member from the other.

The man standing in front of her was short and rather rotund, his belly making the material stretch out in front of him. The man he was talking to was taller and had a loud voice. A feminine voice tittered nearby. Mrs. Robertson, she decided, but she couldn't pick her out of the sea of white in front of her. She heard Red Thompson's loud voice from across the room and picked him out of the crowd. He was talking to Ted Rogers, whose voice she recognized as well. She would keep her eyes on those two. They were the ones responsible for Tony's disappearance.

Another ghostly figure suddenly appeared at Andrea's elbow and she giggled in spite of herself. It was Mr. Robertson. She recognized him in a second! He wore his old-fashioned, thick-framed glasses over the hood! They perched there precariously, tilted at a severe angle across his face. Andrea could see tiny, neat squares cut out of the material, just above his ears. He must have realized she was looking at him, for Mr. Robertson reached up and adjusted his glasses, squashing the bulky material gathered on his nose.

"These infernal things," he muttered. "They fog up under the hood, but I can't see without them!" He moved on, grumbling as he mashed his glasses into the hood.

Leaning against the wall, Andrea noticed three doors off the main room and then a corridor leading toward the warehouse part of the building. She decided she should check the rooms just in case Tony was there, bound and gagged. Making sure that no one was looking in her direction, she sidled to the nearest door. It was closed. Placing her back against the door, she reached behind her, the metres of material covering her movements. She grasped the knob and slowly turned it. The door slid open under her weight and she turned her head, swiftly sliding into the room and closing the door behind her.

It was dark and empty, just a bare office with a desk and two wooden chairs and a closet. She fairly flew across the room and threw open the closet door. It was full of boxes. They hadn't hidden Tony in here. It was doubtful that they would have brought him into their offices, she realized, because they wouldn't want to be caught. But still she had to check, just in case.

Letting herself out of the room, Andrea closed the door behind her, feeling rather proud. Everyone continued to talk. No one seemed to have noticed her Houdini act. She could spy with the best of them. This brought a slight smile to her lips as she headed toward the next door. Maybe she could perfect the act and do something at her school's Variety Night next spring.

There were two more rooms to check. She put her silly thoughts away and concentrated on the job at hand. Repeating her actions a second time, Andrea discovered another empty room with an empty closet. Frustrated she let herself out of the second room, congratulating herself again. She was getting pretty good at this, she decided, as she leaned her back against the last door. With the ease of confidence, she reached behind her and opened the door and slipped inside shutting herself into the dark room.

"Well, well, well." A sinister sounding voice echoed across the room. "What have we here?" A hand clamped itself onto her shoulder and Andrea yelped in fear as she jumped a metre off the floor.

"What are you looking for?" the voice snarled. It sounded like Mr. Robertson.

"I-I was just looking for the ladies' restroom," Andrea sputtered, going with the first plausible excuse that flew into her head. "I thought it must be in here. I tried all the other rooms."

"So you have," Mr. Robertson replied darkly. "I was watching you." He didn't sound convinced that she was merely searching for the ladies' room. "We don't want any trouble tonight. Let me see your membership card."

Hands shaking badly, Andrea had a terrible time pulling it out of her pocket. Her sweaty fingers got tangled up in the material and stuck like glue. She felt like a fly caught in a giant spiderweb. The heavy outfit, which was furnace-hot inside, hung on her shoulders like a dead weight. Breathing inside the hood was like breathing under a thick blanket and she wondered if she was going to faint from lack of oxygen. She finally managed to pull the card out and fumble it to the man waiting impatiently beside her.

There was the sound of a match being lit. Andrea watched as Mr. Robertson perused the card slowly, his ridiculous glasses reflecting the small flare of light. "Doreen Smith," he read aloud. "I didn't know there were many Smiths in Moose Jaw," he said, suspicion heavy in his voice. "And I don't recognize the street address either. Where do you live?"

Panic grabbed hold of Andrea and shook. Her knees felt weak and she forcibly locked her kneecaps to keep from falling. The door sprang open beside her. "What's going on, dear?"

"I'm getting a bad feeling about this member," Mr. Robertson told his wife.

She looked over at Andrea, then reached up and pulled her hood off. Cool air slid into Andrea's lungs as she stared up at the two ghostly figures.

Mrs. Robertson laughed. "Oh, this is my latest recruit. Sorry, honey," she said, helping Andrea pull the hood back into place. "My husband is too mistrustful. Don't worry about this one," she told him slipping her arm around Andrea's waist. "She's with me tonight. I'll take care of her."

"Now, you be careful of what you're doing," she playfully scolded her husband as she led Andrea out of the room. "We don't want to scare our new recruits away on their first night out, now do we?"

True to her word, Mrs. Robertson stuck to Andrea like Velcro. "Here we go," she told Andrea, tittering in her ear as they joined the larger group moving down the corridor. "We're going into the warehouse and then down to a secret place underground. I bet you've never been into a tunnel before, have you?" Taking Andrea's silence as a no, she continued. "Well, you're going to have an interesting adventure tonight! I hope you aren't the squeamish type."

"Tunnels?" Andrea asked, trying to sound doubtful and afraid. "Why are we going down there?"

Smirking to herself, Andrea celebrated inside as they waited their turn. Maybe it was going to be easier than she thought! And wouldn't Ms. KKK be surprised at what Andrea knew about the tunnels! The line was slow moving and she wondered if it was because people were having trouble seeing through their hoods.

"We keep special things down there. Things we don't want everyone to know about. It's like our secret headquarters." Mrs. Robertson grew silent, allowing Andrea to go first through the doorway.

Andrea followed the group into the warehouse. She recognized the office area situated in the centre of the building as soon as she came through the door. To her right across the floor, she could see the large doors which opened onto Ominica Street. Being back in this warehouse made her shudder. She remembered how it felt being tied up in that very office while the bad guys made plans to do away with her. She vowed to find Tony as quickly as possible.

The crowd wound its way past the office and between stacks of boxes, heading toward the opposite end of the warehouse. They came to the wall and began milling about looking lost. Red Thompson chuckled. "I had you fooled," he laughed, leaning casually against an innocuous-looking shelf. "I'll bet you couldn't find the entrance to the tunnels even if you knew where to look. Anyone want to try?"

Andrea watched as the group grew still. She knew where the tunnel entrance was but knew it was better not to draw attention to herself. There was a shuffling of feet but no one volunteered. Turning toward the wall, Red pulled on the shelf. It glided open silently on well-oiled hinges, revealing a new set of stairs.

There was a gasp of surprise and Red laughed again. "Follow me, but pick up a lantern on your way by." He indicated a low table with several unlit lanterns. "We'll light them once we're underground."

The stairs were wide and easy to descend, even in the awkward costumes. They were new, obviously just built in the last few months. Even so, there was no handrail and Andrea moved cautiously, worried that she might trip on the hem of this ghastly outfit.

At the bottom of the stairs a door stood open. "Welcome to the underworld," Red Thompson said as he waved his arm toward the open door. Andrea stepped through and found herself on the far side of the underground storage area in the southwest corner of the area – near the entrance to the Forbidden tunnel.

Ted Rogers stood near the doorway lighting the lanterns. Shadows danced across the dirt walls and stretched across the floor as people moved further into the storage area. Andrea saw Mrs. Robertson stop to chat with someone behind them. Taking the opportunity, she rudely pushed her way to the front of the line and thrust her lantern at Mr. Rogers.

"Okay, okay, don't get excited," the man cautioned as he lit the lantern. "Stay together," he warned everyone. "You don't want to get lost down here."

The underground storage area looked pretty much the same, Andrea decided, as she pushed her way to the far side of the group and stood slightly away from everyone else. This gave her the chance to study the layout of the area.

Boxes and crates lay piled to the ceiling in a haphazard way. It almost looked like a maze. It was bright enough for her to see the entrance to the tunnel which led to Rosie's house, across the room. Near the Forbidden tunnel beams of wood were propped up against the wall. With a gasp Andrea realized that these were crosses.

"Oh, there you are," a voice commented, and Andrea nearly jumped out of her skin. Mrs. Robertson laughed. "This place is a bit frightening, isn't it?"

Was she threatening her in a roundabout way? Andrea wondered, glad of the hood for once. It gave her the chance to stare and look around without being too obvious, awkward though it was staring out of the two small eyeholes.

Red Thompson called for attention and the group pushed closer together. With all the white, they looked like a herd of sheep, Andrea decided. She held back so that she ended up on the outskirts of the group. The people in the back leaned against a big stack of boxes. Behind this the Forbidden tunnel loomed. Looking around, she carefully studied the walls. Where could Tony be?

Red Thompson began speaking, explaining why they were using the tunnels and what this underground area was used for. Paying no attention at all, Andrea scanned the walls, wishing she had X-ray vision. Her heartbeat thudded in her ears and she willed herself to stay calm. She had only one chance to find and free Tony and this was it. She couldn't blow it. Where was Tony?

Andrea found her gaze lingering again on the wall near the Forbidden tunnel. What was that? Lifting her lantern higher, she squinted, concentrating. Was there something there, or was her overactive imagination getting the best of her again? She could just make out a shape across the wide expanse. Was that a door?

Not sure what she had seen, Andrea decided to go investigate. She glanced casually at Mrs. Robertson, who appeared to be totally engrossed in what was happening at the front of the group. With a casualness she didn't feel, she turned slowly and edged away from Mrs. Robertson, sliding away until she stood with her back against the stack of boxes. She stayed there for a moment and then nonchalantly reached over and adjusted the flame in her lantern until it sputtered and became a tiny ridge of flame.

Glancing over at Mrs. Robertson one last time, Andrea made her move. With the swiftness of a cheetah, or at least she hoped it was, she slid behind the boxes and was out of sight of the group.

Andrea flew toward the pile of crosses, her eyes scanning the spot. Yes! It was a door. Turning, she saw that no one was following her. She could see the glow from the lanterns outlining the boxes and hear Red Thompson still talking. Thank goodness he was long-winded. Swiftly, Andrea reached out for the knob and turned it. Letting herself into the room, she swiftly closed the door behind her.

The small flame from her lantern gave next to no light and Andrea couldn't tell where she was. The room felt small, claustrophobic, in fact. Something shuffled and moved in the corner and she stifled a scream. "Tony?"

Remembering her lantern, she fumbled with the small screw and light jumped into the room. There on the floor, hog-tied and gagged, lay Tony, horror written all over his face. "Tony!" she whispered, energy sluicing through her body. She dropped to her knees, her arms aching to hug him. Tony jerked roughly away from her.

"Oh," Andrea suddenly remembered and pulled the hood off. "It's me. Andrea," she giggled nervously.

Relief washed over Tony's face and his eyes lit up.

Carefully Andrea pulled the gag out of his mouth. "Are you okay?"

He nodded, running his tongue across dry, cracked lips. "Untie me," he croaked. He whipped around presenting his back to her. "Boy, am I glad to see you!" He burst out, happiness dancing in his soul. Then he remembered. "We need to get out of here now. Those guys were waiting until later tonight and then they said they were going to 'dispose' of me." Tony shuddered.

"We're not home free yet," Andrea said between clenched teeth as she fumbled with the ropes. They were tied tightly, the cords digging into Tony's wrists and ankles. "I can't do it," she muttered, mentally kicking herself for not having thought to bring scissors. She lifted the lantern and glanced quickly around. The room was as small as a closet, a tiny workroom of sorts. A bench had been built across the wall. On it she could see something shiny glinting in the light.

Tripping on the long costume, Andrea lurched to her feet, holding the lantern high. "A knife!" she said. She grabbed it and dropped to her knees behind Tony.

"Be careful," he muttered. "Don't stab me with that thing, but hurry!"

She cut the cords on his hands first, the knife easily slicing through the thickness. He rubbed his wrists while she attacked the rope around his ankles. "Done." Setting the knife back on the bench with a clatter, she stood.

"We haven't got much time. There are about twenty people out there. I don't know how we're going to escape. Mr. Wong and Vance are waiting for us to lead these people through the Forbidden tunnel and into the Windy tunnel near the Hazelton Hotel, but I don't see how we can do it."

A grin flashed across Tony's face as he felt adrenalin pumping through his veins. "Are you wearing anything under that stupid costume?"

"Of course, I've got my jeans and sweatshirt on," she replied, impatient with Tony's silly question. "But what's that got to do with anything?"

"Well, take the costume off and follow me! We're going to lead them on a wild goose chase they'll never forget!"

Tony waited a few seconds while Andrea quickly shed the outfit, letting it drop to the floor with a muffled sound. "Ready?"

Andrea nodded, "But what if they don't follow us?"

"Oh, but they will," Tony said, certainty ringing in his voice. Holding up his hands in the light Andrea saw two long sticks. "I'll bang these together."

Another idea jumped into Andrea's head. Grabbing another long stick, she picked the hood up and pushed the stick inside and then waved it over her head like a ghoulish banner. "This ought to get some attention," she grinned. "Ready, Tony?"

"Yeah," Tony smiled back. "You shine the lantern

and wave that hood around, and we're off."

Andrea opened the door. Red Thompson was still talking, but the people were beginning to mill about. She could see that about half the group was already leaving via the wooden staircase. One man carried a cross. She wondered where they were going. The other group was listening to final instructions. They were growing restless, shifting this way and that, their feet making scuffling noises in the dirt.

Andrea and Tony crept past the crosses to the entrance to the Forbidden tunnel. No one had heard them or seen them yet; the pile of boxes hid them from view. They could have easily snuck away, never to be heard of again, but that wasn't part of their plan. "Hey! Over here!" Tony called out, clacking the sticks together. "I'm over here! Bet you can't catch me!"

People gasped in surprise. Red Thompson craned his head around the boxes. "Well, go after them!" he yelled. "That kid's a spy!" and the group sprang into action.

Andrea and Tony dived into the Forbidden tunnel, heading south. Even with the lantern it felt claustrophobic. The walls closed in around them, the light from the lantern causing a hideous shadow dance on the walls as they ran. They could hear yelling and cursing behind them and the sound of many feet tramping on the ground. This tunnel gave Andrea the creeps and she willed herself not to remember the time a hand had reached out of the darkness and grabbed her, scaring her so much she nearly jumped out of her skin! She still had nightmares about that horrible event.

When it seemed they had been running for an eternity, they suddenly burst out of the tunnel and into a wider area. They were now in the tunnel which led to the train station. "We better slow down," Tony huffed beside her. "We don't want to lose them."

They jogged slowly ahead and stopped at the entrance to the Main Street tunnel, which led east under Main Street and into the Windy tunnel. The noises grew louder behind them. "There they are! Get them!"

Grinning, Andrea and Tony jumped into the Main Street tunnel. It was lower, but that didn't matter to either one of them, they were short. At the intersection of tunnels, they turned north into the Windy tunnel and sprinted on. "I hope Vance and Mr. Wong are here," Andrea panted, peering ahead, feeling a faint sense of panic. "I don't see them."

"Me either," Tony gasped, "but they'll be there. I'd bet my life on it."

We may be betting our lives on it, Andrea thought. She didn't know how much longer she could keep running and the Klansmen behind her were beginning to gain ground.

Suddenly something moved. Up ahead they could dimly see Mr. Wong and Vance standing in a pool of light. "Hurry!" They mimed, waving frantically.

With a final burst of energy, Andrea and Tony reached Mr. Wong. He handed them off to Vance, who practically shoved them into the tunnel, which led to the Hazelton Hotel. "Go home," he ordered shortly, barely sparing them a glance. "Mr. Wong and I have business to take care of."

Ignoring Vance's command, Andrea and Tony stood just inside the tunnel entrance and watched as Vance and Mr. Wong crouched in the darkness, ready for action. The Klansmen, unaware of what awaited them, ran on full tilt, their lanterns sputtering.

Suddenly many loud thuds filled the air, followed by grunts and groans. White-draped figures flew in all directions. "Hey! What's going on?" one of the Klansmen called out, threatening the air with a long stick. Andrea recognized Ted's voice. Mr. Wong leaped into the air, his left leg extending outward, and kicked the stick out of Ted's hands, the force knocking the man to the ground.

"What's going on?" he cried. "I'm getting out of here!"

"Me too!" Mr. Robertson called, his glasses dangling from the right earhole. "Wait for me!"

Ted whirled around, dragging Mr. Robertson with him. They raced away in the opposite direction, their ghostly attire billowing out around them as they ran side by side back down the Windy tunnel. In their haste to escape, they roughly pushed the other Klansmen aside, knocking them down as effectively as a runaway bowling ball down a narrow alley.

"Hurray!" Andrea and Tony cheered, jumping up and down in excitement, their heads touching the top of the tunnel.

"Way to go!" Tony called, rushing out to shake Mr. Wong's hand. "You did an awesome job!"

"Thank you, Tony," Mr. Wong replied, looking back down the tunnels where several white figures were laid flat out on the tunnel floor. "Vance and I just started this," he commented. "I think those horrible men took care of themselves."

Everyone laughed as they scooted quickly through the short tunnel to the rickety old staircase. They climbed up the stairs to the door at the top. It sprang open under their weight and they stumbled out into the dark street beside the Hazelton Hotel.

"Whew," Tony gasped, leaning against the wall, trying to catch his breath. "Thanks for rescuing me, everyone. I was really, really worried."

Now Andrea knew what parents felt like when their kids did something dangerous. Part of her wanted to strangle Tony until he promised never to do anything stupid again. The other part of her needed to touch him to make sure he was all right. She gathered him closely to her and rested her chin on the top of his head. "I was really scared too. I'm glad you're safe now."

"Me too," Vance and Mr. Wong echoed, dusting themselves off.

Mr. Wong waved goodbye and hurried away. "My family will be worried. I must show them that I am all right."

"I'll walk you partway," Vance said, patting Tony and Andrea on the shoulder and then catching up to Mr. Wong. "I have a story or two to write! Wish me luck, you two!"

"Good luck," Andrea and Tony chorused, "and thanks again." They watched until the two heroes turned the corner and disappeared down Main Street."

"I'm exhausted," Tony sighed. "Let's go home – I mean back to Rosie's. You know, in some ways it does feel like home."

"I know," Andrea smiled, "because in lots of ways, it is home, in the present and in the past." Her thoughts turned to Grandpa then and a wave of worry washed over her. Would she ever get that notebook and get back to the future?

PITCHING IN

Footsteps clattered up the stairs and Andrea awoke with a start. Opening her eyes, she found she was lying in Rosie's bed. Rosie was asleep beside her, an arm thrown over her eyes to ward off the light. It was late morning; the sun beamed into the window bright and warm.

It had been late when Andrea and Tony had returned to Rosie's. They had checked on Sarah and found Beanie asleep on the couch. Rather than wake her, Andrea had lain down on Rosie's bed, thinking that she would move when Rosie returned. She must have fallen into a deep sleep, for when Rosie got back home in the wee hours of the morning, she had just climbed in beside Andrea and gone to sleep as well.

The kitchen door banged open. "Rosie! I got the

paper! Come look!" Beanie's voice called. "Your article's on the front page of the paper and look at the photograph! Hey! Rise and shine, you sleepyheads!"

Rosie stirred beside Andrea. "Just a minute," she said, her voice groggy and hoarse. "I'll be right there."

"Good morning," Andrea smiled over at Rosie. She jumped into her rumpled jeans and sweatshirt, which lay scattered on the floor at her feet. "I'm going to go check on Sarah."

Sarah was up and in the kitchen, already preparing breakfast for everyone, Vance hovering beside her. "I'm sorry I was such a nuisance last night," she said to Andrea as she came into the kitchen.

"You weren't a nuisance," Andrea retorted. Giving Sarah a hug, she was careful to avoid her bandaged arm. "You were hurt and scared and in shock."

"You tell her, Andrea. She thinks she gave everyone too much trouble," Vance mocked softly, shaking his head at her. "How could Sarah ever be trouble? Except right now!" He added in exasperation as he tried to gently drag her away from the stove. "I don't think you should be up and around so quickly. You should be resting!"

"I'm fine, Vance," Sarah said, refusing to budge. "Really. I feel so useless in bed, even if I am awkward with my bandaged arm. Just let me be." She swatted at him with her good arm. "Go check the paper! Beanie's waiting."

"Yes, I am," Beanie asserted, hiding the paper behind her back as Vance playfully tried to grab it from her. "I won't show it until everyone is here, so hurry up!"

"You're looking better," Andrea decided, studying Sarah carefully. There was colour in her face this morning and her eyes were bright. "I'd say you're back to your old self again." She wanted to ask about the notebook, but she didn't dare. She decided, though, that she would look for it as soon as she got the opportunity.

"Yes, I am better," Sarah said.

Tony had gotten Alan up and they sat playing quietly on the floor. "Morning, Andrea," Tony greeted her, his manner subdued. "I'm sorry about last night," he said. "I know I had everyone worried."

Andrea playfully tweaked Tony's hair before bending down to kiss Alan. "You're safe, Tony. That's all that matters." She watched as he played with Alan. "You know, you'll have to think about taking the babysitting course next year when you're twelve. You're really good with kids."

Tony's face lit up. "Thanks, Andrea, I'll think about that!"

Rosie came out of the bedroom in her housecoat. "Let's see that article."

"Finally," Beanie sighed. She spread the paper out over the kitchen table and eagerly pointed. "Look!"

she said. Andrea and Rosie crowded around to get a glimpse. Vance merely scowled at the newspaper before taking Tony's place on the floor with Alan.

The photograph of Wong's Café showed all of the windows blown out, leaving yawning holes in the wooden frames. Rosie's headline read: *Wong's Café Attacked!* And in smaller print: *Who Would Commit Such a Dastardly Deed?*

"It's a good article," Tony said, skimming quickly through the details.

"Did Vance's article make it into the paper?" Rosie asked, casting worried glances in his direction.

"Yes," Vance muttered unhappily as Beanie quickly flipped through the pages. "It's on page five."

While Rosie's article covered Mr. Wong and Sarah and the attack on the café, Vance's smaller article took a different slant on the events of last night. He had interviewed the police officers and reported on their investigation into this crime, as well as the broken window at Rosie's house.

"It's good too," Tony asserted, returning to play with baby Alan.

"Yeah, but it's not on the front page," Vance groused, aimlessly stacking up the wooden blocks for Alan to knock down.

"Really, Vance," Beanie pointed out, her hands on her hips, her voice impatient. "You have an article published in the paper! That's more than anyone else can say. So what if it's on page five and not the front page! You've only just started this career. Be proud of yourself. I'm happy for you."

"I'm proud of you, Vance," Rosie said, stifling a yawn.

"Me too," Sarah and Andrea said in unison. Vance just glowered at them.

"Hey! Tell everyone what a hero you are," Tony piped up, grinning at Vance. "Tell us about you and Mr. Wong."

Vance grinned. "Those Klansmen never knew what hit them. You should have seen Mr. Wong in action!"

"Yeah," Tony interrupted. "He did some of those fancy karate kicks, like this!" He kicked his leg out, almost knocking over a chair. "Those white-sheeted guys were falling all over the place! They didn't know what hit 'em!"

"Mr. Wong was dressed in black and they couldn't see him until too late," Andrea added.

"The men near the back thought it was a ghost! They hightailed it out of the tunnels and kept running. I don't think they'll ever come back!" Vance laughed and the others joined in.

"Can you believe it?" Tony shook his head. "And I thought the guys in those white costumes looked more like ghosts."

"How's the café looking?" Andrea asked.

"I don't know," Beanie replied. "Vance and I are on our way down there now. We just thought we'd stop off here first and show Rosie the newspaper article."

"I want to go too," Tony said, "but I need to eat first. Wait for me?"

Remembering his diabetes, Beanie nodded, grinning. "Sure I can wait. I was hoping you'd want to go and Andrea too. I think they could use our help cleaning up that mess. And I'd better remember to bring that hat," she added, more to herself than to the others. Picking Red Thompson's hat up from the shelf near the window, she plunked it down by the door.

"It's a good thing we found it," Tony added. "Some detectives we'd make, misplacing the evidence."

"It was just under Alan's bed," Beanie pointed out. "It must have gotten kicked there by mistake, but at least we have it now."

"Okay, breakfast is ready," Sarah said, awkwardly putting the food on the table with her good arm. "You all eat up and then get to Mr. Wong's. I'll take care of Alan, since I can't do much else." Agreeing, they quickly pulled up chairs and began to eat, eager to be off.

"Whew, this is hard work," Tony said, brushing sweat off his forehead as he surveyed the cafe. He leaned on his broom, taking a break.

"I need a breather too," Beanie said, coming up beside him. She carried a box in her hands. It was full of pieces of glass, both large and small.

"How many trips have you made out to the garbage bin with that box full?" Tony wondered.

"I don't know, but we're not even half done here yet," Beanie sighed, surveying the mess.

Glass had blown everywhere. It covered every table and chair, every shelf and countertop. "Do you think we'll ever get this mess cleaned up?" Andrea groaned. Her back ached from bending over so much. She carried a box similar to Beanie's, only bigger. Her job was to pick up the bigger shards, leaving most of the smaller ones for Beanie.

They all wore thick gloves to protect their hands. These had been donated by the general store just down Main Street. As well, several other townsfolk were helping with the cleanup.

Mrs. Wong moved among them offering drinks. She was grateful for their help and a little teary-eyed at times.

Mr. Wong had taken a special shine to Tony and showed him how to help clean the cooking area and utensils. Proudly, Tony did the work. "It's my way of thanking Mr. Wong for saving me," Tony whispered to Andrea when she came by to see what he was doing.

Vance and several other men were busy cleaning the window frames of the old glass and then carefully putting in the new windows. "I don't know when we will be able to pay you," Mrs. Wong fretted, wringing her hands as she watched them work.

"Don't worry about it," Mr. Paterson said, wiping his face with his handkerchief. "We're just neighbours helping out other neighbours." It was a Saturday and he was dressed in overalls and a plaid shirt. He looked very different than when he was dressed in his police uniform, and Tony stifled a grin.

"Look at your dad," he whispered to Beanie, when she came close. "He looks like he could be a tunnel runner!" They giggled behind their hands.

"What's so funny, you two?" he called out playfully, when he noticed them. "Do I have two heads?" He wiggled his ears.

"Hey! How do you do that?" Tony wondered, trying to wiggle his own.

"It's magic," Mr. Paterson laughed, going back to work.

Mr. Samborsky, a lanky older man with greying hair, helped set a large pane of glass in place. "He owns the hardware store down the street," Beanie pointed out. "His helper, Mr. Popoff, and his wife Anya just had a baby. They said I could watch the baby for them sometimes."

A couple of other men were clerks in the bank. Mr. Deschamps and Mr. Brossart were cleaning the glass out of the next window frame and readying it for the next large pane of glass. "Wow, you have a lot of great neighbours," Tony decided.

Rosie and Viola smiled and then went back to work washing a myriad of dishes. "I can't believe how many plates and cups a restaurant has!" Rosie exclaimed. "We may be here all night!"

"Here come a few more volunteers," Viola pointed.

Andrea turned to look. "Oh," she said in surprise, feeling her face grow warm. "It's Maria, isn't it? And Tymko?"

"Yes." Maria looked suspiciously at Andrea. "I thought you were joining–"

"No," Andrea quickly interrupted her as Viola frowned. "It was all a mistake."

"A misunderstanding, you mean," Vance said, coming over and patting Andrea's shoulder. "She was just doing a little investigating for me. She was never serious about joining that despicable organization!"

"Oh, I'm so relieved to hear that," Viola smiled.

"As am I," Maria added, slipping her arm through Andrea's. "Now we can be friends!"

Cleaning up the glass turned out to be an all-day affair for everyone. "It's amazing the amount of this stuff we've carted out of here," Andrea commented, going by with yet another full box. "They're lucky most of the food was in covered containers, or they'd need to replace all of that, too." Every item in the cafe needed to be washed and rinsed thoroughly, especially the dishes.

It was twilight by the time the work was finished. Exhausted, everyone sat in the now clean booths, resting before they went home. "I will cook for you," Mrs. Wong said, waving at them. "You will have supper here."

There were several nods of approval and a few cheers, but Viola hushed them. "Yes, we will eat here," she agreed loudly, "since the dishes are clean." Several people laughed at her joke. "But why not make it a potluck supper? Everyone go home, get cleaned up, get your families, and bring one dish back."

"What a good idea," Mr. Samborsky called out. "My wife and I will bring perogies. She was making them when I left home."

"We'll bring borscht," Mr. Popoff chimed in. "My wife makes the best borscht in Saskatchewan!"

Several other people began to offer ideas and suggestions. "We'll meet back in an hour," Viola called over the happy din and the people began to disperse.

Andrea watched as Maria and Tymko hurried away, wondering what they would bring. She was glad that they now knew the truth about her.

"I'll go get Sarah," Vance offered, coming up to his mother. "She's probably wondering what's been going on all day." Taking off his gloves, he walked toward the door. "May I take your car, Rosie?" he asked.

"Sure," Rosie agreed easily, slipping off her shoes as she sank into a booth. "I don't think Sarah should walk that far."

Andrea slid into a booth and sighed in relief looking out the new glass windows. A car drove slowly past the café going down River Street toward Main. She idly watched it as she sipped her soda. The man in the passenger seat was gazing intently into the restaurant, a sneer on his face.

Sitting for the first time in hours, Andrea let her weary limbs relax. Her mind wandered and she wondered how Sarah had managed all day with Alan. Tony and Beanie slid into the bench on the other side of the table.

A sound came from outside and the same car chugged past slowly, this time travelling west on River Street. Andrea realized with alarm that Red Thompson was driving the car! He slowed right down to a crawl. It was as if he were looking for someone in the café.

"Quick! Duck!" She called, kicking at Tony with the toe of her shoe as she slid under the table and onto the floor. Tony and Beanie did the same.

"What's going on?" Tony asked, a worried look on his face.

"A car just cruised by really slowly. It was Red Thompson. I'm sure he's looking for both of us!"

"Well, he's not looking for me," Beanie commented. She sat up straight again and stared out the window.

Andrea wasn't surprised to hear the car make a third drive-by in almost as many minutes.

"Something strange is going on here," she said, waving to get Officer Paterson's attention, forgetting that she and Tony were still crouched beneath the table.

"What is it?" he asked, coming across the room to stand beside her. He bent down to peer at her. "Did you lose something?"

"See that car? Just turning on to Main Street?" Beanie pointed out the window.

"That's the third time it's driven by," Andrea added, still on the floor, her head bent at an awkward angle. "It's always going very slowly, and it's being driven by Red Thompson, one of the leaders of the KKK."

"Is that so?" Officer Paterson rocked back on his heels. Andrea could almost see the little wheels in his mind spinning as he assessed the situation. "Well, I'll just wander outside. If they go by again, I'll have a little talk with them. I've been wanting to ask them some questions anyway. I've just been too busy to track them down. It looks like they might have saved me the trouble." He turned to Beanie.

"Did you bring that hat you found in the street, like I asked you to? I'm going plant a little bait. Don't you worry," he added as Beanie pointed to the hat on a table across the room. "We're safe here. I don't think they'd try anything with all of us inside."

Moving quickly, Officer Paterson stepped out of the door and then slipped into the shadows and disappeared. He was good at his job, Andrea decided.

She scanned the area but couldn't see him, even though she knew he was there. She just hoped the car would come by once again.

Curious and feeling braver, Andrea and Tony crept up onto the seats and looked outside. The car had tried to creep by again, but this time Officer Paterson was there. He was standing directly in front of the automobile, impeding its progress, the hat hanging limply from his fingers. Stepping up to the driver's side, he leaned in to talk to the occupants, his hands resting on the door frame with the hat.

Noticing what was going on, several of the other police officers left the restaurant and ambled over to the car, lending Officer Paterson their support. They all watched as he beckoned for the occupants of the car to get out.

"That's the man who kidnapped me," Tony said excitedly, pointing to the driver, who was now standing beside the car.

"I know, that's Ted Rogers and Red Thompson." Andrea quickly filled the other two in on what had been happening. "I can't understand why they would be driving by like that. It's almost as if they wanted to be caught."

"Or they've been looking for us and hoped they'd find us out and alone." Tony shivered. "I'm glad we're safe inside."

"They probably didn't realize the police would be

here helping," Beanie guessed. "After all, they sure don't look like policemen, dressed in their overalls."

"Maybe they were going to try breaking all the windows again and were just waiting for everyone to leave," Tony said.

"Maybe," Andrea said doubtfully. She didn't think they'd be that dense.

The voices from outside grew loud and angry and the other police officers moved in closer. "I'm glad there's extra help out there," Rosie said, looking worried. "I don't like the looks of those two men."

"What's Officer Paterson doing with the hat?" Tony wondered aloud.

They watched as he let it swing loosely in his hand as if it wasn't there. "Look at Red Thompson," Andrea giggled. Try as he might, he couldn't keep his eyes away from the hat. His head swung this way and that as Officer Paterson turned the hat. "It's so obvious it's his hat."

"I'm sure he's wondering why Pa doesn't just ask him about it so he can deny it," Beanie snickered.

"I'll bet that's one of his strategies," Tony surmised with satisfaction. He loved watching his great-grandfather while he worked. "Look how uncomfortable Red Thompson looks, even from here! I'll bet he's just sweating, wondering when the axe is going to fall! He's bursting to deny the hat is his and he isn't being given the chance!"

"That's strange police work," Andrea commented, a little smile playing on her lips. "But it seems to be working!"

Just then Vance pulled up in Rosie's car. "Oh no," Rosie gasped. "I hope they don't see Sarah."

"I hope they do," Mrs. Paterson said, leaning over the table and peering out of the window. "I want them to know that they hurt someone – why, they could have killed her! And the Wongs too!"

Officer Paterson waved with the hat and the men scrambled quickly back into their car. They pulled away, squealing their tires as they turned the corner.

Watching them go, Officer Paterson followed the others back into the café. Shaking his head, he rejoined the group, placing the hat in the middle of the table. "I think we've got our men," he told them. "You should have seen that red-headed man sweat! He was so nervous! And I pulled this out of the back seat." In the palm of his hand was a scrap of paper.

"That looks like the same writing that was on the note attached to the rock at my house," Rosie said.

With a gasp, Beanie reached quickly into her pocket. "That looks like the paper I found in the warehouse. I forgot I had it until now."

Beanie blushed beet red when she realized what she had said. She stammered, trying to think of a plausible explanation for being in the warehouse. Officer Paterson merely raised his eyebrows and looked pointedly at her as if to say, "I'll deal with you later."

"What does the note say?" someone asked.

Officer Paterson peered at it. "'Coolies, get out of town now if you know what's good for you,'" he read. "Well, that's very compelling evidence." He tucked the note into his breast pocket. "It looks like those men have some more explaining to do."

THE BRAWL!

It was well into the evening by the time the food was served. "I'm starving," Tony exclaimed, digging into his plate full of fried rice and stir-fried vegetables, perogies, salad, and scalloped potatoes, with a side bowl of borscht and sour cream. He figured he'd come back for seconds and have the quiche and crepes for dessert. It was a multicultural extravaganza with more food than a hundred people could eat.

"This is the best potluck food I've ever tasted," Andrea seconded with her mouth full.

Everyone else was too busy eating to comment. The café was very quiet as the people consumed the delicious food. The only sounds were of forks scraping against plates and water glasses being set down with a light thump.

In the quiet of the room, Mr. Wong stood, his eyes shining. "I want to thank my dear neighbours and good friends," he began, his voice choked with emotion. "You have helped us through a terrifying experience. In that moment when the rocks were coming through the window, I thought that I would die. I worried about Miss Sarah and my family. I worried that maybe many people hated the Chinese because our skin is a different colour and our eyes are a different shape."

He smiled out at the people, his eyes filling with tears of gratitude. "I can see now that I didn't need to be worried about this. You have restored my faith in people. Thank you."

Everyone put down their utensils and clapped as Mr. Wong put his palms together in the middle of his chest and bowed low. "Thank you, my friends," he said again.

Mrs. Paterson dabbed at her eyes with her serviette. "That poor man. How would it feel to know that people didn't like you because of your skin colour! I'm glad we all showed him that's not true for everyone."

"Yes," Rosie agreed. "Maybe if we all stick together, we can help eliminate discrimination in this world."

Andrea stayed silent, wishing them luck. She didn't want them to know that even in the present, racism was still a problem. Clearing her plate, she declined a third helping and went to stack dishes. Many people were already in the kitchen helping wash, dry, and put the dishes away. Grabbing a tray, she went back to her table and helped pick up the last of the dirty dishes.

"You go home now," Mrs. Wong said, smiling at the Patersons and their whole group, which included Andrea, Tony, Rosie, Alan, Vance, Beanie, and Sarah. She took the tray from Andrea. "The baby is tired. He needs his sleep."

"Yes, he does," Rosie agreed, scooting out of the bench seat. She took Alan from Viola's arms and he nestled his head into his mother's shoulder, closing his eyes and tucking his thumb into his mouth.

It was lucky they had two cars. Andrea didn't think they would all have fit into one, and she didn't want to be one of the ones walking home. It had been an exhausting day and she was dead on her feet.

"You can drive," Rosie said to Vance as they crossed River Street, nearing the parked cars. "I'm too tired."

"Why don't you come with us?" Viola invited, linking arms with Rosie and patting the sleeping baby on the head. "We'll let the children take the other car."

"Sure," Rosie easily agreed.

"I have to stop at the police station for a minute, if that's all right," Constable Paterson said, helping Rosie into the back seat of his car. "It won't take long, though."

As everyone else piled into Rosie's car, the first car

took off, heading west toward First Avenue. "All aboard," Vance called. Tony, Beanie, and Andrea scrambled into the back seat behind Sarah. Putting the car into gear, Vance pulled a U-turn in the middle of the deserted street and at the corner, turned left onto Main Street.

It was a silent ride home, each person comfortably drowsy from all of the good food and hard work. Each was dreaming of a nice soft bed awaiting them just a few short minutes away. The car moved along Main Street, the tires humming. Abruptly Andrea's thoughts jumped to Grandpa Vance and she wondered again how he was doing.

As the car turned the corner in front of the Klan office, it suddenly skidded to a halt, throwing everyone in the back seat onto the floor.

"Hey! What's going on?" Tony sputtered. Strange thumping and pounding noises were coming from down the street, followed by grunts and groans and long strings of swear words.

"Oh, my goodness," Sarah gasped, peering ahead into the darkness.

In the glare of headlights, they could see a large group of grown men punching and hitting one another. It was an all-out brawl! The doors to the warehouse flew open and more men spilled out into the night, fighting and jabbing one another. Some men were even wrestling on the ground, moaning and groaning as the punches made contact with soft flesh.

Loud curses and yelling filled the air.

"What's happening?" Beanie questioned, her hands gripping the back of Vance's seat.

"There's a fight going on in front of the warehouse! There must be a dozen men out there!" Vance estimated.

"Look," Andrea pointed out. "There's Mean-Eyed Max!"

"Yeah," Tony added, standing up on the back seat to get a better view. "He's punching out that red-headed guy! And Chubbs and Stilts are fighting his friend!"

"Mr. Thompson and Mr. Rogers," Andrea supplied.

"Can you believe it, these guys are fighting a block away from the police station!"

"It looks like the Klansmen have discovered the missing money and Mean-Eyed Max, too! We need the police!" Hurriedly, Vance backed the car up and then careened up Main Street. At the next corner, he turned left, the car tires squealing in protest.

At the police station, Vance braked sharply, and leaving the car idling, jumped out. "I'll go get help!" He raced up the cement stairs and threw open the heavy door, disappearing inside.

It took less than a minute for the police to mobilize. A large number of police officers came pouring out of the station, their billy clubs raised. Some raced down the street on foot while others hopped into vehicles and drove down the block to the fight.

Vance came out of the station last and climbed back into the car. "They can sure get organized quickly."

"Should you go home now?" Mrs. Paterson questioned, her eyes disbelieving. "Is it safe? The fighting is still going on down the street. It's practically at your doorstep!"

"You're all under arrest!" echoed loudly up the length of the block. The noises and curses faded slightly and then tapered off as the police began to gather up the men and handcuff them.

"I think we're safe now," Beanie reported proudly. "My pa's got everything under control."

"Do we have them all?" They heard a voice ask. "I thought there were more men than this."

The arrested men were walked up the street to jail. Silently they passed the cars, still parked in front of the station. Some muttered swear words under their breath as the policemen walked beside them.

Only Mean-Eyed Max was still being unruly, pushing and shoving to get at Chubbs and Stilts. "I told you to take the money and run," he seethed, lunging across a nervous police officer to get at the other two. They shrank away from him, fending off his blows with their shoulders.

Everyone in the car sat rigid as the policemen and the bad guys marched past. "I don't see the red-headed guy, or his friend," Tony hissed, carefully watching the group.

Mean-Eyed Max overheard him and glared in his direction. "You're lucky I got arrested, kid, or it would have been curtains for you. I would have found you somehow."

Tony shrank back against the seat, his breath trapped in his throat. He had blocked that horrible event out of his mind and now Mean-Eyed Max had reminded him.

"What was that about?" Vance questioned. "He was threatening you!"

"I know," Tony replied. "The Klansmen were going to let Mean-Eyed Max take care of me. They said he'd killed another kid before and left his body behind the Hazelton Hotel."

Vance gasped. "They mean Jack!"

"You can go home now," Officer Paterson interrupted, coming up to the two cars. "I think I'll be quite a while," he said, smiling apologetically at his wife. Rosie had moved to the front seat and was preparing to drive Viola home.

"Listen," Vance said, quickly starting the other car and heading down the street for Rosie's house. "I'm going to drop you all off and go back to get a story. I'm going to try to question Mean-Eyed Max. If he did kill Jack, then I want him punished for it."

"Wait for me, Vance," Rosie called as the car began

to drive away. "I'll take Beanie and your mother home and join you there." Beanie hopped into the automobile Rosie was driving.

Vance nodded as everyone settled back in the car for the short drive home. They clambered out of the car while it idled in front of the empty house. Tony was the last one. "Look for the red-headed guy, Vance," he begged as he shut the passenger door. "I'm sure he got away. We should be out looking for him. He probably took the money and ran!"

Giving him a hard stare, Vance ordered, "You stay here with Sarah and Andrea! I don't want you or Beanie involved in this – understand?"

Nodding unhappily, Tony trudged slowly up the stairs, his head down. "Boy," he groused, stomping his way into the kitchen. "Vance sure knows how to take all the fun out of everything!" He flung himself into a chair and folded his arms across his chest. "So do you, Andrea!"

Sarah had gone straight to her apartment after Andrea convinced her that she was perfectly capable of putting Alan to bed alone. This left Andrea and Tony free to talk.

Andrea cradled a sleepy Alan in her arms as she hovered near his bedroom door. "Sh-h-h," she admonished as she rocked the baby. "You'll wake him up."

Ignoring her, Tony continued. "We should be out looking for those bad guys and you know it! They're going to get away with all that money and it'll be our fault! I'll bet they're on their way to the train station right now! Come on, Andrea! Leave the baby with Sarah and let's go! We can catch them!"

Slipping silently into Alan's room, Andrea put him in his bed and covered him up. Coming out of his room, she shut the door behind her. She remained quiet for a moment, thinking about what Tony had said. Was he right? What was their responsibility in all this mess?

A picture of Grandpa, pale and sick, flashed into her mind. "Our job is to get that notebook and get back to the present as soon as possible," she reminded him. "I know where that notebook is and I'm not going to waste my time chasing some bad guys around. We're not even sure the men are missing. Anyway, you should think about being more careful, especially after we just rescued you!"

The fight ran out of Tony like a deflating balloon. "You might be right," he said. "I'd just hate to see all that money disappear and those guys get away with it."

"The people gave the money for a bad cause anyway," Andrea reminded him, flopping into a chair beside him. "If we did rescue the money, we'd only be helping to promote hatred and discrimination, since it would probably go back to the Klan membership. I sure don't want to do that!"

"No, I guess I don't either," Tony agreed. "But I'll

bet you anything the money and those men are missing in the morning." He moved toward the bedroom. "I'm going to bed."

Watching him suspiciously, Andrea warned, "Don't you go sneaking out tonight, Tony. I couldn't handle it." Her voice broke as her throat clogged with unshed tears of worry and frustration. "I can't be worried about you when I'm so worried about Grandpa and getting that notebook. Please don't do anything dangerous," she pleaded.

Hearing the worry in her voice, Tony came back and stood patting her shoulder. "I promise, I won't," he agreed, even though this hadn't been his original plan. When she looked doubtfully at him, he added. "You know me, Andrea. When I make a promise, I keep it. I don't want you to be worried. I know how upset you've been over all of this, especially my getting kidnapped. Heck, I'm still in shock over that too!"

Andrea took a deep breath. "Thanks, Tony. I know you'll keep your word." She hugged him tightly for a moment. "I'm glad you're my brother," she said gruffly and then released him. "Go to bed now, but don't wake up Alan. I'm going to see if that notebook is still at Sarah's."

Sarah was already in bed when Andrea entered the apartment. She moved around the small living room and kitchen area like an undercover agent, spying in all the corners, under chairs, and in cupboards, looking for the notebook. After a twenty-minute search, she admitted defeat. Sarah probably had the notebook in the bedroom. That didn't do her any good at all.

Feeling dejected, Andrea stretched out on Sarah's couch, pulled the blanket up, and tucked it under her arms. Perhaps tomorrow luck would shine on her and she would find the notebook. Then they could return to the present. The constant worry and stress over Grandpa weighed heavily on her. She wanted to be with him now. What if she never saw him again?

Vance's Big Moment

"It looks like Tony was right," Rosie commented as everyone assembled in her kitchen bright and early the following morning.

"I knew it!" Tony interrupted. Pumping the air with his fists, he did a little dance around the kitchen.

"I didn't see a red-headed man or his friend in the cells last night," Rosie continued, smiling indulgently as Tony pranced by. "And from the story Mean-Eyed Max and his friends were telling, the two who escaped during the arrest got away with a large sum of money.

"Vance did some late-night investigation and asked questions about Jack too, but no one is talking. When I left the newspaper office early this morning, he was just writing an article about the red-headed man and the money."

"See, I told you," Tony said, but his words were without sting. He had figured out, after a restless night, that Andrea was right. Their main concern was helping Grandpa, not rescuing a bunch of money for the KKK. Anyway, what was done was done. It was up to the police to figure things out from here.

"At least they caught the other bad guys," Andrea said, looking comfortable from her spot on the floor where she was playing with Alan. She felt comfortable too, in her own clothes. She was tired of wearing dresses and had opted to put on her jeans and sweatshirt this morning instead.

At that moment Vance came bounding up the stairs waving the rolled-up newspaper over his head like a banner. "I'm on the front page!" he shouted, a huge grin on his face. Dancing around the room, he swooped Sarah off her feet, planting a loud smacking kiss on her lips.

"Yuck," Tony said, wiping his own lips on his sleeve.

"Careful there, Tony," Rosie teased, feinting left in a mock attempt to kiss him. "I might have to do the same to you."

Covering his face with his hands, Tony ran to the other side of the room, narrowly evading her outstretched arms.

"Let me see the article," Sarah cried, hugging Vance excitedly and then grabbing the newspaper from him. "Let me see!"

Everyone crowded around the table while Sarah eagerly spread the paper out. The headline was in bold black letters: LEADERS OF THE KLAN DISAPPEAR ALONG WITH THE MEMBERSHIP MONEY, BY VANCE TALBOT. "I'll read it aloud," Sarah said, her voice full of pride.

A late night investigation by this reporter and the police has led police to believe that the two main leaders of the Ku Klux Klan have absconded with a large sum of money. It is believed that during a brawl on Ominica Street last night, the leaders managed to evade police and make off with an undisclosed amount of cash. That is, if the word of Mr. Maxwell (a.k.a. Mean-Eyed Max) is to be believed.

The police theorize that the two managed to escape during the arrests and weren't missed until several hours later when Mr. Maxwell complained about losing a large amount of money at the scene of the brawl. The police and the reporter returned to the scene of the crime, but found little there but a few loose buttons from dress shirts and large clumps of human hair.

There were no leads as to where the two have disappeared, although there is speculation that they may have returned to the United States. Anyone with information on the whereabouts of these two men is asked to contact the police, as they are continuing their investigation.

"Oh, Vance," Sarah gushed, her cheeks bright red. "This is wonderful!"

Glowing with pride, Vance bowed to enthusiastic applause from his relatives. "It's about time," Rosie declared, giving him a bear hug and then thumping him on the back. "You got top billing this time! My article is only on the fifth page." They all laughed, remembering how upset Vance had been when the situation had been reversed.

Vance grabbed Sarah up in his arms and kissed her soundly. "I've been given a raise and a small promotion with the paper. This means we can get hitched soon!"

Tony gagged behind his hands and Andrea whacked him on the shoulder. "Sorry," he said, scowling. "I just can't believe they're going to get married so young!"

Vance kissed Sarah again and danced her once around the room. Then he grabbed Andrea and waltzed away with her. "Hey! You can come to the wedding! How many grandchildren can say that they attended their grandparents' wedding?" Throwing his head back, he laughed, nearly knocking Andrea off her feet.

"I'd love to," Andrea said, excited at the thought. Then common sense took over, engulfing her in a melancholy haze as she remembered that she had a job to do. She had to find that notebook and get back to the present. Grandpa was waiting for her.

"But we'll have to buy you some new clothes." Vance continued cheerfully. As he let her go, he pulled playfully at the moose on her sweatshirt. "I don't think you'd want to wear this to the wedding." Turning, he caught Rosie up to dance with her as Beanie grabbed Alan and whirled him around the room.

"You could be the belle of the ball, Andrea! We'll invite all of our friends and family to meet you two." His eyes twinkled merrily. "We just won't tell them that you're our grandchildren!" He started making a mental list of guests.

"I have only one regret," Vance added, his eyes clouding over.

"I know," Sarah said softly, her eyes sad. She came to stand behind him, reaching up to squeeze his shoulder with her good arm.

"What's that?" Andrea wanted to know.

"I started working at the newspaper just after Jack died. I vowed that somehow, through the investigating that reporters do, I'd find out who killed him." Vance sighed, emotion brimming in his eyes. "I'm no closer to finding his killer than I was when I started. I feel like I've let Jack down."

"It was Mean-Eyed Max and his gang," Tony said. "I heard the Klansmen talking about it."

"They wouldn't have lied to each other," Andrea assured him. "Not about that, anyway."

Vance looked pensive for a moment, his face full of sorrow. Grabbing his hat, he turned to Sarah. "Where's my notebook? I have to go do something."

"It's in my bedroom," Sarah said, moving across the room.

"I need it." Vance followed her out the door.

Startled, Andrea felt her head reel. What was Vance up to? Why did he suddenly want the notebook? Intuition screamed at her to follow Vance. If she didn't, she might lose the only chance of getting her hands on that notebook.

While Vance and Sarah went downstairs to Sarah's rooms, Andrea quickly motioned to Tony. Dutifully, he trotted over and plunked himself down on the floor with Alan. "Hiya, buddy," he greeted, patting his head. "Is Andrea getting tired of playing with you?"

"I'm going to follow Vance," Andrea bent forward and whispered in Tony's ear. "I'm worried he's going to hide that notebook and we'll never be able to get it. You'll have to cover for me."

Rosie and Beanie were still busy poring over the newspaper as Alan swatted his blocks across the floor. "But what do I say?" Tony sputtered, looking very alarmed.

Shrugging her shoulders, Andrea stood up and sidled to the door. "I don't know, but you'll have to think of something!"

WHERE'S THE NOTEBOOK?

Creeping silently down the stairs, Andrea could hear Vance and Sarah talking quietly as they walked into her apartment. Knowing she had very little time, Andrea slipped silently past the doorway. Once at the front door, she pushed it open. Rosie's car was parked on the street, and without thinking, she dove into the back seat and crouched low. She didn't know if Vance would take the car or not, but if he did, she wanted to be right there with him.

Andrea heard the front door to the house thud against the door frame. Footsteps pounded down the wooden steps, then clomped toward the car. The door opened and the car sagged as Vance climbed inside. It roared to life and pulled away with a lurch that sent her flying against the back seat. She tried to right herself, but found nothing to hang onto. The leather of the back seat was slippery and offered her little to grip. She settled down, sitting with her legs folded under her, trying to wedge her body between the seats.

The uneasy feeling Andrea had felt was slowly increasing in the pit of her stomach. It caused her limbs to tingle and made the tiny hairs on her arms stand upright. What was going on?

Vance drove very fast. The street was bumpy and the car seemed to hit every rut. Once or twice, Andrea found herself bouncing so high she was sure her head must be visible over the seat! Just when she thought she couldn't take any more pain, the car slowed and Vance pulled over and stopped, cutting the engine. He seemed to reach for something on the passenger seat and then climbed out of the car. A swishing noise caught Andrea's attention and she wondered where they were.

Peering over the edge of the car, she saw the huge expanse of prairie stretching to the western horizon. Where were they and where was Vance? She turned her head back towards the town. A square of white picket fence marked out a tiny cemetery. Vance had come to visit Jack's grave.

Opening the door, Andrea quietly crawled out of the car. Closing the door as quietly as possible, she crouched low and headed for a lone tree that grew just outside the cemetery. Vance was only one row away, his back to her, and she sighed with relief. She didn't want him to find her here during his private moments.

Secure behind the tree, Andrea cautiously poked out her head. Vance was sitting on the ground beside a cement marker. Squinting, she could just make out the name "Jack." Vance appeared to be reading from his notebook. She couldn't hear Vance's words, although his voice drifted on the breeze now and then.

How long Vance read, Andrea wasn't sure. She let her mind wander, wondering what he was reading. Was he saying a final goodbye to Jack? Was he apologizing for not being able to find his killer? She wondered, too, why Grandpa had never talked about his writing. And she worried about him too. Getting this notebook was taking a lot longer than she had anticipated. She rubbed her arms, feeling her hair still standing soldier-straight. What was the matter with her?

A sudden noise startled Andrea out of her reverie. Vance had stumbled to his feet, wiping his face on his shirt sleeve. Turning around swiftly, he stared toward the tree. She shrank back against it, hoping he hadn't seen her. She heard the swish of grass as he came near and wondered how he had found her! What excuse could she give him for invading his privacy?

At the last second, Vance veered away. When she dared look around the tree again, she saw him lugging a large stone toward Jack's grave. He dropped the stone with a loud thudding noise and fell to his knees. Scooping at a natural depression near the headstone, Vance dug a hole in the earth. When it was deep enough, he picked up the notebook and dropped it into the hole.

Quickly covering it with earth, he moved the stone on top and stood dusting his hands off. "I'm sorry I couldn't help you, Jack. I'm leaving you a gift. Goodbye." He whirled away and walked back to the car.

Shrinking against the trunk of the tree, Andrea stayed motionless as the car started up and rattled away. She watched it move toward town, becoming smaller and smaller, until it was a speck in the distance. Even then she didn't move. Did Grandpa really mean for her to take the notebook? It felt as if she would be stealing something precious!

A sense of urgency began to press at her heart, making her head spin. She could feel a squeezing in her chest. It was the feeling that told her she had to do the job and she'd better do it now. She had to get that notebook. The tunnel was calling her. It was time to get back to the future.

Had something happened to Grandpa? Not even daring to think past that thought, Andrea went after the notebook.

Resolutely, feeling like a thief, she climbed the fence. In her haste, her left pant leg caught on a picket and she scraped herself. It smarted painfully. Rubbing the sore spot, she hurried to the graveside, bent down, and tugged at the stone. It didn't move. She tried again, this time putting more energy into it. The stone wouldn't budge. What had Vance done, cemented it in place?

The sense of urgency seemed to swell within her and she pushed with all her might. The rock wobbled and then fell back in place. Almost panicky now, she wondered how she would ever get the notebook out.

An idea popped into her head. She needed a lever; something to pry the stone up with. Tall, dry prairie grass met her gaze in every direction. Where would she find something? Then she remembered the tree. Running toward it, she saw a dead branch on the ground beneath it. It was long and about ten centimetres at its thickest. It might do.

Using the stick, Andrea pried the rock up. It moved and then rolled to the side. Heaving a huge sigh of relief, she scooped out the dirt and found the notebook. Shaking the earth from between its pages, she tucked the notebook into the waistband of her jeans. She pulled her grimy sweatshirt down to hide it and then somehow managed to roll the stone back into place. She hoped Vance would never come looking for his notebook, because he sure wouldn't find it.

The need to return to the present filled her being. Now that she had the notebook, there was nothing keeping them here. The desire to see her grandfather overwhelmed her. Andrea set out running toward town. She didn't know how long it would take her, but she had to hurry. How ironic that would be, she thought, if they somehow missed getting into the tunnel.

Running, gasping for breath, she tried to calm herself. Worry wouldn't help anything, but she couldn't stop it from filtering into her mind. Her throat burned and a painful ache developed in her side. She clutched it as she ran, hoping the pang would ease. Her leg hurt from the scrape and her calves were sore.

When Andrea thought she couldn't run one step further, the first buildings of the town appeared. The sight renewed her energy and she raced on, the need to get to the tunnel pressing on her. How much time did they have?

The town was a blur as she rushed through it. Turning onto Main Street, she raced on, bumping into people, almost knocking an elderly man into the street. "Sorry," she called over her shoulder as she sped on. Ominica Street came into view and she turned. Rosie's tall house loomed ahead and she turned in through the gate. Bounding up the stairs, she collapsed in a heap at the door, gasping for breath.

"What happened?!" Sarah asked, rushing to her side.

"W-we have to go," Andrea managed.

Tony was at her side in an instant. "It's time?"

Andrea nodded. "Now," she gasped. "I can feel it." Rushing over, she hugged Beanie, Vance, Sarah, Rosie, and Alan goodbye without speaking. Part of her was glad it was happening this way. She didn't want to explain why she was so upset, or take the chance of anyone seeing the notebook.

"Are you sure you're all right?" Vance asked, giving her a look of concern.

Andrea fell into his embrace, almost weeping out loud. "I'm sure," she whispered, a few tears falling on his shoulder. She had the urge to tell him about the notebook and everything, but she knew she couldn't do that.

"I was hoping you could stay for the wedding," Sarah sighed. "I wanted you to be my attendant."

"Wouldn't that be something," Tony laughed. "Are you sure we can't stay, Andrea? It'd be so much fun!"

"Tony!" Andrea wailed, tears springing to her eyes. "I'd like to stay too, but you know we have to go!" She'd thought he understood.

He nodded, a sheepish look on his face. "I know." He stooped to give Alan one more kiss on the forehead, then stood up and raced toward the bedroom to grab his knapsack, his fanny pack secured around his waist, as usual.

"Okay, I'm ready."

Silence descended as the whole group stood looking at one another around the crowded kitchen. Impulsively, they came together in a group hug near the kitchen door. There were a few sniffles and tears, some emotional laughter, and more hugs.

"It's been great," Vance said, cuffing Tony playfully on the head.

"Just like always," Beanie added, leaning into Andrea.

"Yes," Rosie agreed.

The pull of the tunnel tugged insistently at Andrea, reminding her that it was time to go. Gently, she disentangled herself from her wonderful friends.

"Goodbye," she said softly, taking Tony by the hand. Her eyelashes sparkled with tears. "I love all of you."

"We love you too," they all chimed in, moving toward the doorway to see them off.

"Don't come with us," Andrea said, following Tony toward the stairs. "We don't want to attract too much attention when we slip into the cellar door around back."

"You'll have trouble lifting that heavy door," Vance reminded them. "I'll come and see you safely in."

Without looking back, Andrea and Tony quickly descended the stairs and went out the front door, Vance following closely behind. Andrea barely noticed that the window in the door had been replaced. They hurried around to the backyard. Casting furtive looks around, Vance pulled the heavy cellar door open.

"In you go," he said, holding the cellar door up.

Andrea and Tony scrambled into the darkness, their feet clomping on the wooden steps. Sunlight slanted across the wall and they looked back to see Vance silhouetted against the brightness of the daylight.

He touched two fingers to the brim of his hat in a salute. "Take good care of yourselves."

"We will," they promised, and the door dropped shut behind them.

Tunnels of Surprise

Andrea pushed open the door in the wall and stepped into the tunnel. It was pitch black and the air smelled stale and dank. "The lanterns aren't lit," she commented. She felt as if she were being pulled into a black hole.

"I've got a flashlight," Tony remembered. Andrea heard the rustle of the canvas and then the rasp of the zipper and the light clicked on. Instantly light pooled at their feet. Aiming the flashlight down the tunnel, they rushed along silently, side by side. Each lantern they passed was cold, little cobwebs already stretching across some of the glass panels.

"I guess all the bad guys are really gone," Tony said.

"Maybe Constable Paterson has finally succeeded in chasing them all out of Moose Jaw," Andrea agreed, as the beam of light bounced ahead of them. It outlined the entrance to the storage area, giving it an eerie glow. "Hey," she muttered, stopping dead in her tracks.

"What's wrong?" Tony asked, bumping into her. "More ghosts?" He laughed nervously, peering into the murky darkness.

"I thought I saw something," Andrea murmured. She carefully scanned the entrance for a moment. "I guess I was mistaken. Come on, let's go." She grabbed Tony's hand.

Ghosts still invading his mind, Tony jumped, stifling a scream. The flashlight slid from his nerveless fingers. It dropped to the floor with a thud, rolled down the tunnel, and then went out.

"Oh no," he moaned, dropping to his knees. "Help me find my flashlight." He scurried like a cat stalking prey, down the tunnel, blindly reaching out, his fingers skimming pebbles and dirt. "Andrea? Help m–"

"Look, Tony," Andrea interrupted, her voice urgent, "I did see something! There's light coming from the storage area! I wonder what's happening? You wait here, while I go have a quick look."

"No!" Tony hissed. "Remember what you told me. Let's just find my flashlight and get out of here!"

"I have a funny feeling about this. I think I should go investigate, it might be important. Wait for me."

"It's not a goo–" Tony sputtered, but Andrea was gone.

Working her way silently down the dark tunnel, she stretched her arms out, her fingers brushing the dirt walls. The light grew brighter as she crept along. Faint noises echoed through the tunnel, coming from the storage area, and she wondered what was going on. Reaching the entrance, Andrea peered in.

The boxes, which had been stacked neatly, were now strewn haphazardly around the area. The pamphlets and billowy Klan uniforms littered the ground.

A movement caught Andrea's eye and she looked over to find Stilts rifling through a box, frantically searching for something. Emptying the contents, he swore, tossing the crate carelessly behind him. It landed with a loud crash. "I can't find it!" He called, reaching for another box.

Who's he talking to? Andrea wondered, too late. An arm snaked out of the shadows and grabbed her by the hair.

"Got ya, girlie!" A voice growled and Andrea's heart sank to her toes, as Chubbs whirled her around, a smirk on his face.

"Let go of me!" she shouted loudly, hoping Tony would hear her. Chubbs laughed and twisted harder, pulling her up onto her tiptoes. The notebook pressed against her stomach as tears spurted in her eyes. Oh, why hadn't she left well enough alone?

"You and your friends sure caused a lot of trouble for us, girl," Chubbs rasped. "We're out of jail now, and the judge thinks we're coming to court in a few days. We have other ideas."

"Quiet," Stilts ordered, standing over the two of them, a big stick in his hand. "Don't blab so much. Let me think. What are we going to do with her?"

"Let's just get what we came for and get on the train," Chubbs said. "We'll tie her up and leave her here."

"She could die down here," Stilts said, his voice faltering.

"So what? She's messing around in our business again!" Chubbs gave a yank on her hair and Andrea yelped in pain.

"I-I wouldn't tell anyone," she said as butterflies dive-bombed inside her stomach. "I promise."

"Why would we trust you?" Chubbs retorted. "You're not getting off scot-free, kiddo!" He grinned menacingly at Andrea.

"Well, I'm not killing nobody," Stilts said flatly. "'Specially not a girl. That's not what I do. Sheesh, I still get nightmares about that other kid."

"That wasn't our fault," Chubbs said. "We didn't know Mean-Eyed Max would pull a gun. He probably just meant to scare the kid."

They were talking about Jack, Andrea realized with a start.

"I wrestled with Max, but the gun went off...it was too late." Stilts stared into the gloom, his eyes reflecting the horror as he relived that moment. "It wasn't my fault. I tried to stop him..."

Suddenly an eerie white shape floated into view in the storage area. "I am the ghost of death," a hoarse voice breathed. "I have come to seek revenge!"

Chubbs and Stilts stood frozen on the spot, their mouths hanging open in terror. "B-but we didn't mean for him to die!" Chubbs sputtered.

"It wasn't our fault!" Stilts whimpered.

The ghostly image seemed to swoop in on them. "I am the ghost of death! You must pay the ultimate price! You must die!" The words echoed through the storage area as Chubbs and Stilts both screamed. They threw up their hands and then dived into the Forbidden tunnel, yelling in horror. Their shrieks reverberated off the tunnel walls, growing softer and softer.

Andrea doubled over with laughter. The white Klan hood fluttered to the ground as Tony stepped out from behind some crates and took a bow. "Not a bad performance, eh?"

"You were great," Andrea managed. "I'm sure they won't stop running until they reach the border! Come on, let's get out of here. Now we can tell Grandpa for certain what really happened to Jack."

"Well done, young Tony," a different voice added, and Andrea and Tony jumped.

Mr. Wong stepped into the circle of light spilling

from the lantern. "I thought I would have to interfere and save Miss Andrea, but Tony has done an admirable job. I am proud of you!" He chuckled. "I saw those two characters leave the police station and I followed them. I had a feeling they were up to no good, and I was right!"

Picking up the lantern, he walked around the scattered boxes, coming to stand where Chubbs and Stilts had been. "They were searching for something and I don't believe they found it."

"What?" Tony asked, peering over Mr. Wong's shoulder as he pried the lid off another box.

Holding the lantern high, Mr. Wong rummaged through the neatly folded Klan uniforms. "Aha!" He smiled, holding up a small sack.

"Hey!" Tony recognized it. "That's the sack of money those guys took from the Klansmen."

"Exactly." Mr. Wong smiled. "I had a feeling, when I followed them here, that money might be involved. I was thinking that we might use this money to help the families who were so rudely treated, especially the family that lost their laundry business to the Klan. What do you think?"

"That's a wonderful idea," Andrea smiled. "I hope they'll be happy coming back."

"Yes, and they will see that there are many people in Moose Jaw who are friendly to them, regardless of race or colour," Mr. Wong added. "And now I must go. I will deliver this money to them right away." He weighed the bag in his hand. "I think there will even be enough to help a few more families, and this is good."

"Yeah," Tony agreed. "I can't think of a better way to spend all that membership money the Klan collected."

"After all, we can't give it back," Andrea seconded.

"Goodbye," they called to one another as Mr. Wong disappeared up the stairs.

He smiled back at them once. "Good luck in the future!"

Electricity seemed to pulse in the air as they came closer and closer to the tunnel that would lead them back to the armoire and, ultimately, the present, where they belonged. Tentacles of time reached out to them, surrounding them, drawing them home.

"I'm happy to be going back," Andrea whispered as the force pulled at her clothes, but she felt sad, too, to be leaving her good friends. She patted the notebook, reassured by its presence, glad that she had accomplished the mission for Grandpa.

The world began to spin around them. Words whirled out of her mouth as she felt her body begin to float in space. Lights flashed and spun around her until they blurred together into one brilliant light. She felt as if she had just been shot out of a superpowered cannon, heading for outer space.

Slowly, the world began to right itself and Andrea found herself standing with Tony on the steps outside the armoire. It was slowly moving away from the wall to allow their entrance back into Grandpa Talbot's office and the present. Her thoughts immediately flew to Grandpa and she felt for the notebook. Good, it was still there.

A Wonderful Life

It was hard to believe that they'd only left the hospital a little over two hours ago, in this time. So much had happened to them. That awful antiseptic smell engulfed them as soon as they entered the building. The place seemed busier, with orderlies pushing gurneys around and nurses and doctors hurrying down the long corridors.

The elevators moved at a snail's pace and Andrea tapped her foot impatiently, the notebook clutched in her hand. Now that she was back in the present, she only wanted to be at Grandpa's side, showing him the book, hoping that it would somehow provide the cure he needed to get well again.

Finally, the elevator reached the floor and its doors whisked open. "Andrea! Tony!" Aunt Bea exclaimed as they stepped onto the floor. Her cold fingers pressed into Andrea's free hand.

"Oh my goodness, is that...is it Vance's notebook from so long ago? I'm so glad you found it," she said, taking the book and hugging it carefully against her chest. "I thought this was lost, never to be found again! I didn't ever ask Vance what he'd done with it. He never wanted to talk about it after he and Sarah got married."

"How is he?" Andrea asked. It was the only thought, the only question on her mind.

Aunt Bea sighed, blinking back tears. "He's holding his own, dear." She dabbed a handkerchief under her eyes.

"When can we see him?" Andrea asked, eager, impatient, and scared all at the same time.

"Soon," Aunt Bea promised. "Your parents are in the room with your grandma just now."

As if on cue, the door opened and the three stepped out, Grandma in front looking stoic, her face ashen. "He's asking for you, dear," she said, addressing Andrea. "He keeps asking for that –" she stopped speaking in surprise, her eyes resting on the worn notebook in Andrea's hands, then she smiled, huge tears rolling down her cheeks. "You've got it!" she exclaimed.

Grandma's hands reached for the notebook and she clasped it to her lips, breathing in the scent of it. "He never told me until years later what he'd done with it.

I'm glad you managed to stop him from burying it. You'll have to tell me all about it, but later. Go to him first, he'll want to know." Tenderly, she handed the notebook back.

Andrea's parents came up, one on each side of her. Biting her lips Andrea stood, looking first at her mother, and then her father. "I had to do it," she whispered, tears overflowing and spilling down her cheeks. "I had to see him." Sobbing, she hurled herself into their arms.

Both parents hugged her, fighting back tears.

"You could have taken the bus," her mother gently reminded her.

"I didn't even think of that," Andrea admitted. "All I could think of was getting here as quickly as possible. I'm sorry."

"We'll talk about it later," her father said, his voice gruff. "Right now, go see your grandpa."

Taking a huge breath, Andrea steeled herself against all the emotions warring within her, pushed open the door, and stepped into the dim hospital room.

Grandpa lay as before, looking deathly white, his cheeks hollow, his lips chapped and slightly open. His breathing was sporadic, with long pauses between gasps, and wheezing sounds that made Andrea cringe with fear. Tubes seemed to be hooked up to every part of his body and lights and monitors blinked and beeped incessantly.

Approaching the bed, Andrea found herself looking into washed-out blue eyes, a sad imitation of Grandpa's usually vivid eye colour. "Hi, Grandpa," she whispered, her voice hoarse and catching in her throat. "Look what I brought you." She carefully laid the notebook in his hands, which rested on top of the thin white blanket.

Grandpa smiled and his eyes seemed to regain some of their colour; suddenly he had a bit more energy. Caressing the notebook with one hand, he reached for Andrea with the other. Her cold, clammy fingers felt warm in his familiar grasp.

"Thank you," he sighed. "I've regretted all my life what I did with this notebook."

Andrea caressed the back of his hand. "Don't talk, Grandpa. Just rest and get better soon."

"I need to know how you managed to get the notebook back," he asked, sounding so much like his old self that Andrea felt certain he was getting better.

Andrea smiled. "I followed you to the cemetery and watched you bury it. I dug it up when you left." But these details didn't seem important to her now. She wanted to tell Grandpa to save his energy for getting well again.

"Good for you," Grandpa said, chuckling. "I suppose shifting that rock must have given you a bit of trouble."

"It did," Andrea agreed.

"I did go back for it, you know, many years later, but a lot of work had been done tidying the cemetery. Both the rock and the notebook were gone."

"So I was your only hope," Andrea said.

Grandpa squeezed her hand and his eyes twinkled for a brief moment. "I knew I could count on you." A look of pain filled his eyes.

"My only other regret is that I never found out what happened to Jack." He sighed.

"But I did!" Andrea took his hand in hers. "He was grabbed by Mean-Eyed Max and his gang. There was a scuffle and the gun went off, killing him. It was an accident, Grandpa. They really didn't mean to shoot him, they just wanted to scare him."

Grandpa smiled. "Thank you, my dear." His eyes became lively, and then he coughed. It was a chest-rattling sound that seemed to take every ounce of energy he had left.

"Please don't die." The words burst out of Andrea's lips before she could stop them. Her eyes filled with tears as Grandpa painfully coughed, his chest heaving. "Don't leave me."

"We don't get to pick our time," he breathed as Andrea bent closer in order to catch every word. "I've led a wonderful life. I even got to meet my grandchildren when I was in my teens." He smiled at this and seemed to rally a bit.

"And I'll always be with you, dear, even if you can't

see me. Watch for me, listen for me. I'll be in the sound of the wind blowing through the treetops and in the beautiful sunset. I'll be in the sound of children's laughter or the touch of soft rain on your face. I'll always be with you." He reached out and touched her hand.

"But how will I know it's you, Grandpa?" Tears spilled down her face.

He squeezed her hand and pulled her toward him, pressing his lips against her wet cheek. "You'll feel it inside. You'll know." Releasing her, he pushed the notebook into her hands. "I wanted you to have this. Maybe someday you'll be a writer."

"Me?" Andrea asked, bewildered. "I thought you sent me back in time to find a cure or something that would make you well again. I thought the secret must be in this book."

Shaking his head, Grandpa coughed again. "There is no cure for old age, my dear. We are all mortal and we all die. I've been blessed to have lived such a healthy life for so long." He stopped to breathe again and Andrea waited, tenderly stroking his cheek. "I wanted you to have the book. Read it. Read the poems and stories in there. They were meant to be shared and I never let anyone but your grandmother read them. I've regretted that. Read it, but add to it, too."

"Okay," Andrea agreed as she clutched the notebook to her chest. Even in this heart-wrenching situation, somehow she felt stronger and at peace, at least a little bit. "I love you, Grandpa Vance," she whispered, reaching over to kiss his cheek. "I will be watching for you. You better be there!"

"I will," he smiled. "You can trust me on that." He sounded so much like young Vance that she had to smile.

"That's my girl," he added, when he saw the smile hovering on her lips, then waved her off with a weak hand. "Go tell everyone to come in."

THE WHOLE FAMILY was assembled around Grandpa Talbot's hospital bed. Grandma stood next to the bed, her aged hands clutching his. Aunt Bea was on the other side. Tony stood with Andrea at the foot of the bed. She could feel her father's hand on her shoulder offering comfort. The room was full of Talbot relatives.

Waves of sadness engulfed Andrea, accompanied by a feeling of uselessness. Was there nothing she could do? The notebook grew heavy in her hands and suddenly she knew what her job was. This was why she had gone back in time in the first place, wasn't it?

"I found something of Grandpa's," she began, hoping that no one would ask her where she had discovered it. Carefully opening the book, its spine cracking, she turned to the first page and began to read...

This is the journal and writing notebook of Vance Alister Talbot. Dated September 24, 1925. I hereby swear to write only the truth, as I see it, for the truth is many-faceted, like a diamond. In this lowly notebook I will record my deepest thoughts and feelings.

First, I must ask myself, what is writing? How is it that a person may take something as intangible as words and string them together to make something? Suddenly these thoughts and words take on meaning; make a picture in one's imagination; evoke emotion.

Writing starts with an idea. What is an idea but a thought, a puff of energy in the brain? It could vanish at any second, and be gone, like the hundreds of thoughts a person has each day. But by writing the ideas down on a flimsy piece of paper they become something concrete and yet not concrete at all, for they are merely strokes of my pen. How can strokes of a pen make a story?

It is a miracle every time a story happens, because it would be easy not *to write the thoughts and ideas down, but to let them vanish into thin air, never to be recorded. The miracle of writing is this: that someone like me takes the chance and writes his thoughts, hoping to have the opportunity to share a story or poem or idea with the world. And this, in turn, might help make someone happy; or at least give a reader the chance to feel something.*

These are the kinds of thoughts you will find recorded in this notebook. Strange, you might think, but if you are at all interested, please read on...

ACKNOWLEDGEMENTS

Thanks to Barbara Sapergia, Children's Editor at Coteau Books, for all her help and suggestions. Many thanks to the staff of Coteau Books for dedication and enthusiasm. And heartfelt gratitude and appreciation to the first readers of the manuscript, my family and friends, whose continued love, support, and encouragement means so much.

ABOUT THE AUTHOR

MARY HARELKIN BISHOP is a teacher in the Saskatoon Public School system. Her first book, *Tunnels of Time*, which came out in 2000, is one of the fastest selling juvenile fiction titles in Coteau's history. Her exciting sequels, *Tunnels of Terror* (2001) and *Tunnels of Treachery* (2003), were also runaway successes. In addition to her fiction writing for children, Mary has published poetry and short fiction in the Courtney Milne book *Prairie Dreams* and in *Green's Magazine*.

Mary was born in Michigan, but has lived in Saskatoon since 1970.